Blink Twice If You Love Me

Blink Twice If You Love Me

A Crickley Creek Romance

Laurie Beach

TULE
PUBLISHING

Blink Twice If You Love Me

Tule Publishing First Printing, July 2023

The Tule Publishing, Inc.

First Publication by Tule Publishing 2023

Cover design by Erin Dameron-Hill

ISBN: 978-1-959988-57-1

Dedication

This book is for every girl who
feels like she isn't enough.

Chapter One

IT WAS FINALLY her turn. Krista had been dating Rye Smithson since her sophomore year in high school when he saw her at a football game. He asked her to be his date to the senior prom right there on the spot. He even let her borrow a dress from his sister. She fashioned a yellow boutonniere from her neighbor's rose garden, and polished her mother's white shoes until the black scuffs no longer showed.

She knew how lucky she was to be going with one of the Smithson boys—her family didn't have the best reputation in Crickley Creek. And in a town this small, a bad reputation was a life sentence. It didn't matter that she had a job. It didn't matter that she took classes at the junior college. Anyone who dated her would be bringing about a world of gossip and speculation. And who knew, they might be putting themselves in danger, too. After all, her cousin, Randy, had killed a man. Krista Hassell barely had a single relative who wasn't a drunkard, a cheater, or a criminal. Rye had seen through all that, though. He'd been her boyfriend for going on eight years.

Now here she was, at the finest wedding in all of Crickley, and not as the help either.

Charlotte, Krista's boss at the tea and bookshop, was spinning around the dance floor with her new husband, Will Rushton. They were perfectly in sync, their smiles relaxed as if nothing about the two-hundred-person lavish outdoor wedding had been difficult. Krista knew the truth—she'd seen Charlotte stress over the linens and the cocktails and the chairs and the food and the ceremony and the band and every other detail for the past year. Yet nothing was rushed or difficult on this perfect summer day in the garden of Will's family estate. Krista held Rye's hand underneath the table and took a bite of her salad, taking a moment to appreciate the scent that the light breeze had just picked up. It was her favorite, gardenia. She smiled up at him, thrilled that she was the reason they were guests. For once.

"These cheesy potatoes, or whatever the hell these are, ain't half bad," he said, chewing.

Krista beamed. Someday soon, the wedding would be theirs. It would be small, and certainly, Rye's family would pay. But she would be the one in the beautiful white dress, gracefully reciting her vows while her diamond ring sparkled in the sunlight. It was just a matter of him asking.

She squeezed his hand. "Do you want to dance after dinner?"

He laughed. "Naw, you go ahead. I'm thinking of meeting the boys over at the roadhouse for some pool. You can find a ride home, right?"

"Sure." She tried to control the disappointment in her voice. She probably owed him a night out at the roadhouse since he came to the wedding with her. Actually, she owed him quite a bit after leaving him for almost a year. She had been in Myrtle Beach working for a children's charity before she left it all to come back home and help out with her little brother. Of course, she'd seen Rye on the weekends, but he was still struggling to get over the fact that she had it in her to move away from him. He was still making her pay. "I'm sure Birdie or Scruggs can take me home," she said.

"Cool." He stuffed the last bite of filet into his mouth and pulled his phone from his suit jacket pocket. "I can't take much more of this sissy music." His thumbs raced over the screen. "The boys are already there."

Krista sipped her sweet tea and looked away. He'd only just asked, and he was already leaving?

Rye hadn't yet finished chewing. "Give me some sugar." He took the napkin from his lap and threw it on top of his plate of food, then puckered at her. She leaned over and gave him a peck on the lips. He continued chewing afterward.

As soon as he was gone, Krista went to find Birdie. She was easy to spot—big and loud in all the ways: body, voice, opinions, and personality. She even dressed loudly. That evening she'd chosen a sequined dress probably saved from her heyday back in the 1970s, complete with an enormous orange, red, and mustard-yellow floral design. She was sitting next to her new husband, Ashby, whose last name, Crane, described exactly how he looked: like a thin, angular, large-beaked bird.

"Hey, Birdie! Hey, Ashby," Krista said, sitting in a nearby empty seat. "Any chance I can catch a ride home with y'all?" It was a big ask. Krista lived on the marsh side of town. Most people at the Sinclair-Rushton wedding would be living in the nicer, beach side of town.

"We'd be happy to," Ashby answered immediately.

"As long as it doesn't cut into my night of fun," Birdie said. "Ashby's the one doing the driving, anyway. Ain't you, sweet pea?"

Ashby winked at Krista as he uttered, "Yes, dear."

Charlotte and Will had finished their obligatory dances and began working their way around each of the tables, greeting the guests. The sun was beginning to set, and it seemed like every bird, cicada, and bullfrog was singing to welcome the evening. Krista was transported into a warm world of peace and love. Charlotte deserved every bit of the happiness she was clearly feeling. Even though she hailed from California, the beautiful bride had embraced the South—quirks, jerks, and all. She was a good person and earned the true love she'd found. Krista soaked in the moment. One day she might be just as happy. Someday she would be on solid footing, no longer a pariah, no longer having to be grateful for every scrap of kindness someone gave to her. That day would come as soon as her last name changed to Smithson. She smiled to herself, wondering if she would choose the traditional "Wedding March" for her walk down the aisle, or a romantic country song like Charlotte had.

A tall guy with a short military haircut grabbed the microphone and kicked her out of her reverie.

"Whazzup, wedding guests?! Let's hear it for Will and Charlotte Rushton! Hoo-rah!" The man, who was clearly one of Will's old army buddies, began jumping as he motioned for the band to kick up the tempo. "Everybody lift your glasses! It's tequila time!"

The tune switched to "Cotton-Eyed Joe," and despite her age, Birdie jumped up, did a little jig, held her empty water glass to the sky, and yelled, "Bring that tequila over here!" The bride and groom laughed as they headed off the dance floor to their special table.

The man hopped off the stage and proceeded to pour a small portion of the contents of his bottle into Birdie's glass, then he danced his way around the yard, forcing the younger people to join him in his bad idea. He was more obnoxious than a horn-honking clown, but there were plenty of pretty girls eager for what the handsome tequila man was doling out. What was previously a demure and romantic ceremony had just fallen off a cliff into a raucous, cheap, bar-like party.

That idiot is ruining their wedding. Krista sipped her tea and frowned at the scene. Hopefully, Birdie and Ashby would be ready to leave soon.

Even at the best party, or the most interesting dinner, three hours was about as long as Krista could stand. She'd already been there for six by the time the Rushtons' twinkling backyard was finally empty of people. The moon was high and the evening late-night still. She found a pitcher of water on one of the chiffon-covered tables and poured a glass. She'd already scrounged three dinner rolls from Allison Rushton's kitchen, but she'd failed to find any coffee.

She had been left alone with the tequila man, whose name turned out to be Johnny Merrick. When she found him, he was passed out on the grass missing one shiny dress shoe with his head wedged precariously underneath a prickly bougainvillea vine. She'd considered leaving him there, but she'd never forgive herself if she did. So, she risked her cotton evening wrap by placing it between his forehead and the thorns, and gently slid his head away from the danger. He'd been a willing patient, and even sat up afterward, the skin around his forehead, ear, and jawline looking like a kitten had mistaken it for a stuffed mouse.

With a promise of food, she'd managed to get him to walk to a nearby table, where he barely got his rear end onto a chair before slumping forward like a sleepy toddler.

"Here, eat this." She tore small bites and fed them to him. He didn't open his eyes, but he did open his mouth. She got two rolls and a full glass of water into him before he mustered enough strength to open his eyes and look at her.

"Are you Will's cousin?" He smelled of vomit and fearlessness.

"No. I'm Charlotte's friend."

"I thought you were all cousins out here." His words were as slurred as they were ignorant.

She shooed a mosquito away from his sweaty face and immediately regretted it. She should have let it bite him.

"Ya got any teeth?" he asked, squinting at her.

"Teeth?" *Did he just say teeth?*

"Smile at me."

He was lucky she didn't punch him. She glared at him with no hint of a smile. What an asshole.

He chuckled like he was the funniest guy alive and plopped his head back on the table. Two seconds later, he lifted his red, swimming eyes and held them still on her face. Then he pushed himself upright. "You're actually kinda pretty for a backwoods chick."

She poured the remaining water over his head. He immediately shook like a dog, sending droplets all over her. She yelped. Damn him. Struggling to scoot her chair backward on the grass, she finally managed to stand. Birdie could be seen inside the lit-up house, still in the kitchen with the groom's mother, flitting about like it wasn't after midnight and her husband wasn't sound asleep at the table by the giant magnolia. Krista smoothed her skirt and began walking toward the house.

"Don't go," Johnny pleaded. "Can I have your Snapchat? Your Instagram? What was your name again?"

She didn't bother answering him. Who did he think he was? She wasn't even on social media. And that didn't make her *backwoods*, either. That made her smart. Why torture herself by seeing how fabulous everyone else's lives were? Plus, she had no one to be social with besides Rye, her work friends, and Birdie. She walked up the stairs toward the yellow glow of the kitchen. If Birdie wouldn't take her home, she would suck it up and pay for an Uber.

By the time she got to her mother's house, it was almost one thirty in the morning. She waved to Ashby and Birdie before walking along the overgrown crushed oyster shell path toward the chipping, white wood building. The concrete front steps were pockmarked and crumbling from more than fifty years of use, and despite the dark, she knew by heart where to step and where to avoid. She opened the front door quickly to minimize the loud squeaking of the hinges, looking for the only light in the hallway, a night-light both for finding the one bathroom and avoiding any creepy crawlers that had found their way in. There wasn't a family member who hadn't stepped on a snake in their bare feet at some point in their lives, and no one cared to repeat the experience.

Zach was in his room, laid out like a corpse underneath his soft patchwork quilt. She touched his arm to make sure he was still warm. Then she peeked into her mother's room. The bed was empty, the dip in the middle of the mattress a handy hole for the bundled sheets and blankets. Junie had probably snuck out again after putting Zach to bed. There was no telling where she might be—the local bar, a random man's apartment, or sitting fully clothed in a pond filled with alligators. It was the same worry every time, yet somehow Junie always made it home.

"Kiki?" came a hushed voice.

"Hey, bud. Yeah." She walked back to their shared room and flipped on the light.

"How was the wedding?" Zach asked.

He was difficult to hear and understand. The Duchenne muscular dystrophy that had been atrophying his muscles since he was four years old had weakened everything, most distressingly, his lungs. He was only twenty-two, and he could barely move. Krista climbed into bed with him, checking that his oxygen machine was on and functioning.

"The wedding was like it came straight from a magazine," she said. "Miss Charlotte looked prettier than a movie star." Pulling the covers up under his chin, she kissed his cold, gray cheek. "You warm enough?"

"Uh-huh." He struggled for a shallow breath. "Tell me more."

"Well"—she snuggled into his side and stared up at the gray ceiling—"she had magnolias on every table, big, white ones surrounded by peonies in the colors of your favorite Smarties sugar candies. All those flowers, plus Mrs. Rushton's gardenias made the whole place smell like perfume."

"Tell me about the food."

For the past year, Krista and her mother had been feeding Zach through a tube in his stomach. He never complained, but the conversations he enjoyed the most now revolved around food.

"There were two cakes, of course," she began. "Each layer of the bride's cake was a different flavor—vanilla, lemon, hummingbird, and strawberry. I got a strawberry piece, and it was as light as air. The frosting was our favorite kind—buttercream."

He moved his eyes back and forth with excitement.

"The chocolate groom's cake had a layer of frosting so thick and fudgy that it woulda been dessert enough by itself. I didn't have a piece, but from the way Miss Birdalee was *mmmm-hmmmming*, I'd say it was tasty."

Zach giggled, and Krista went on talking about the fantastical dream wedding, embellishing some details and leaving others as the truthful perfection they were. She talked until her brother's eyes closed and her own felt heavier than the weight of their mother's absence. She never, however, mentioned the very drunk, very obnoxious, Johnny Merrick.

Chapter Two

TEA AND TENNYSON was the new hotspot of Crickley Creek. The morning rush for coffee, tea, or all sorts of portable breakfast foods was so intensely chaotic that Krista's newly married boss, Charlotte, had to hire another employee. Krista hadn't taken the time to get to know her, but her longtime coworker, the obnoxious fraternity fool Scruggs Willingham III, put all of his effort into wooing cute little redhead Emma Smith and fully ignored Krista. He just didn't want her judgment. He was the king of the Tea and Tennyson castle, and he expected everyone to know it.

Krista had to admit it was amusing to watch his eyes follow Emma around the store, spending more time thinking of a way to get her attention than actually doing his job. Without words, Krista and Emma had fallen into a pattern of allowing Scruggs's jokes to fall flat by giving him no reaction. He knew they were in cahoots and was losing his patience. All it took was a glance toward each other and Krista and Emma knew the other was laughing inside—not at his joke, but at the fact that they were clearly getting to him.

It was a full house that Monday morning. Krista was the most experienced, so she was behind the counter making the drinks. It didn't matter that there was a line eight people long or that she was hidden behind the loud black espresso machine they'd named Queenie—she was acutely aware of Johnny Merrick's presence the minute he walked through the front door. He was taller than she remembered, and he looked as invincible as a superhero despite the scratches on his chiseled face. His short military haircut, tanned skin, and overconfidence compensated for them. Where was his embarrassment? If she'd been the one making an idiot of herself at a fancy wedding, she'd have been so mortified, she wouldn't leave her house for a month.

He didn't wait in the line. Instead, he walked straight to Krista and leaned over the counter, his face appearing next to the frothing and sputtering machine. "Hey, Krista."

She turned her back and pretended to be completely focused on the nonfat vanilla latte she was assembling.

He pounded on the counter. "Krista!"

She didn't want a scene. "What? I'm busy." How did he know her name? And how did he know where she worked? She picked up the next paper cup in the row and memorized the order on the receipt stuck to the side of it.

"Here." He handed her an envelope. She barely glanced at him, reluctant to take it. He jiggled the card. "Take it."

She sighed loudly, then grabbed the card and stuck it in the front pocket of her apron. There was nothing about

Johnny Merrick that made her want to be nice to him. She'd been around enough drunk men in her life to know that they were a particular brand of male that one would be served well to stay far, far away from.

"You gonna read it?" he asked.

"Yes, later," she said in an effort to get rid of him. He owed her a thank-you for taking care of him and a huge apology for what he'd said. It was possible that a nicely written card might be enough to make her hate him less. Apologies and thank-yous were always nice to get.

He left without ordering anything. Probably needed to go back home and tend to what had to be a massive hangover. Or maybe he was flying back home now that the wedding was over. Either way, it didn't matter.

Admittedly, Krista's mind was stuck on the card in her pocket, which made the morning drag on and on. She had no time to tear it open and read it.

When she was finally free from Queenie long enough to wipe down some tables, she found herself nervous. What if he wrote something inappropriate? Would she have to tell Rye? She wiped a table in the far corner of the store and turned toward the bookshelf for privacy. Then she ripped open the side, avoiding the glued area where his alcohol-soaked tongue had surely licked it closed.

On the front was a beautiful beach scene with a hatching nest of baby sea turtles in the foreground and a pod of dolphins cresting in the deep blue of the ocean behind it. It reminded her of the property her boss had recently inherited, one of the most beautiful spots in all of South Carolina: Katu Island. As an employee and friend of Charlotte's, she was one of the few people allowed on the protected grounds. Charlotte and Will had built a small beach house, and she took Zach there almost every weekend. It was partially hidden in the woods, surrounded by mossy oaks, sea pines, and palmettos.

The classic white cottage had the signature Will Rushton wide wraparound porch and was high enough to look out over the dunes to the Atlantic. Will added a ramp to the back door and built the hallways and bathrooms wheelchair wide. It was the nicest thing anyone had ever done for her and Zach. The home had been completed for only four months, and wasn't completely furnished, but there was something peaceful and spiritual about it. In her mind, she'd named it Serenity. That's how she felt when she was there.

How odd that the card Johnny chose would so intensely spark those memories. She opened it with a smile.

I OWE YOU ONE. CALL ME.

Her smile quickly faded. The man had the audacity to leave his phone number. How rude. He hadn't even properly thanked her. If the front of the card hadn't been so beautiful, she would have put it straight into the nearest trash can. Instead, she put it back in the pocket of her apron. She could tear off his words and place the cover of the card in a frame.

she had her own bookshelf, she would place
. By then she would have forgotten where it
would be free to appreciate the happy scene.

Chapter Three

KRISTA ADDED LOOSE curls to her long, blonde hair, careful not to step on the spot near the commode where the wood was soft with rot. She lined her full lips in light pink and pursed them together with Vaseline to spread the color around, careful to keep everything in her Ziploc makeup bag and not lose it down the old sink that hadn't had a drainage plug as long as she could remember. The bathroom didn't have one inch of counter space, so anybody using the mirror had to put down the yellowing lid of the toilet as a table or balance things on the curved side of the wall-hung sink. There was no room for even the tiniest of tables since their old iron bathtub covered in chipping white porcelain took up most of the space. She leaned in toward the mirror. A little black mascara to make her blue eyes pop, and she was ready to go.

"Bye, Mama! Bye, Zachy!" she yelled as she balanced her way down the front steps, her favorite light yellow sundress blowing in the breeze. She didn't have much in the closet she shared with Zach, but what she had, she took meticulous care of.

Her old baby-blue Ford Mustang was the one good thing left behind from her estranged father. Plopping herself on to the hot blue leather, she drove away from her home by the marsh, away from anyone who knew her. She did this every now and then, convinced that the money spent on gas was worth it. Today, she was going to North Charleston. There was a nice Harris Teeter grocery store there. Not even Rye knew what she was doing. It was too embarrassing to tell even her longtime boyfriend.

When she arrived, she fixed her face in the rearview mirror and fluffed her hair before stepping through the automatic doors into the air-conditioned building and past the line of empty shopping carts. Starting in the bakery, she admired the beautifully decorated cakes, then browsed the aisles, stopping every now and then to read labels. Keeping a slight smile on her face, she made eye contact with the other shoppers, making herself appear open for engagement.

"I love your dress," a woman in the canned goods aisle said.

"Thank you," Krista replied, smiling wider. That was number one.

Not two minutes later, an old woman did a double take. "Well, if you don't look just like an angel, dear."

Krista gave her a brilliant smile in return. "Thank you, ma'am."

Compliment number three didn't come as quickly, but she wasn't ready to leave yet. She still had remnants of feeling invisible and unworthy. There were more people she needed to fool. She saw an opportunity with a stooped old man holding on to his cart like a walker. She hovered nearby, pretending to be choosing between barbecue sauces. Finally, he reached for something and she made her move. "Can I help you with that?"

He looked up at her. "Sure, honey. Thank you."

Krista put the small bottle of ketchup into his basket.

His watery eyes appraised her. "Well, ain't you a purty little thing. Thanks for the help."

"You're welcome." Krista strolled back to the bakery with her head held high. She felt a bit more noticed, special.

At the cake counter, she ordered one cupcake—a chocolate one with buttercream frosting and sugar flowers. Even though he had a feeding tube, Zach could have little tastes of things, so she always tried to find something special to bring home. If Mama was there, they could all sit at the kitchen table or on the back porch by the marsh, and she'd pull off small dissolvable bites for Zach while making sure her mother didn't take more than her allotted third.

She paid with her cash tips and turned to leave, when she spotted something completely unexpected. There, in all her prissy Crickley Creek high-society glory was none other than Virginia Buchanan. What in the hell was she doing all the way out in North Charleston? Krista turned back around, put her cupcake on the counter, and pretended to look at the pies. Of all the places to run into Virginia Buchanan. Didn't her live-in housekeeper do all of the shopping for her? Krista could see Virginia through the reflection on the glass of the pastry cooler. She was dressed in one of her expensive tall and slim pantsuits with her white hair in a French twist and her diamond earrings sparkling like ostentatious engagement rings. She was with a man, a short one with a belly and a noticeable comb-over. The strangest part was, she looked happy to be there.

When Virginia turned the corner, Krista grabbed her cupcake and headed out. A young man walking into the store stopped when he saw her and suddenly forgot what to do with his hands and eyes. She counted that as number four. It felt as good as a compliment.

Since she'd left after work in the afternoon, Krista now had to contend with rush-hour traffic. She was starving, and it was hard not to eat the cupcake on the seat beside her. When she stopped at a light, she texted Rye to tell him she would be late for their dinner date. She lied and said she'd been running an errand for the shop. He'd be annoyed, of course. Until he saw her. Then all would be forgiven.

When she finally got home, Rye's red Hummer was parked in the weeds in front of her house. She walked in the front door feeling lighter and happier, as she always did on the days she searched for compliments. She found Rye and Zach in the kitchen. Zach was working hard, trying to enunciate his words enough for Rye to understand him. In the old days, when Rye first started coming over, Zach would talk for hours about his dream to work for Google or the time he hit a home run or the sailfish he caught when he was ten. Rye used to actually act interested. Nowadays, it was so hard to understand Zach that Rye no longer bothered to look at him when he was talking, just wandered his eyes around like he was bored to death.

"Everything okay?" she said. Zach shot her an apologetic look.

"What is this?" Rye asked. Her black Tea and Tennyson apron was on the kitchen table, and the card that was formerly in the front pocket was now in his hand.

"Oh, that's from a guy at the wedding. I gave him some water when he was drunk." She stood rooted to the floor. There had never been any other guy for Rye to be jealous of. She'd been very careful about that. This confrontation was a first.

"Why would you do that? I leave you alone and the first thing you do is go flirt with some guy?"

"I wasn't flirting. Everybody else had already left, and I had to wait for Birdie and Ashby. The guy was so bad off, somebody had to do something. I was just being nice."

"Nice. Yeah. So nice that...what?" he said, feigning ignorance. "That he feels like it's okay to come into the store looking for you? Give you a card? Like you'd be happy to see him?"

"I wasn't happy to see him. I didn't even think he'd remember me. I just stuck the card in my pocket so he'd leave." She tried to make her voice sound light and innocent.

"Did you call him?" He leaned forward, his wide football player physique as intimidating as an oncoming train.

She took a step backward. "No, I didn't call him. I have no intention of calling him. Just because he *owes me one* and gave me his number does not mean I'm going to call and collect."

Rye's face relaxed, and he leaned into the chair. "Good. I don't like that dickhead."

He didn't even know that dickhead. "Good. I don't like him either." It was true, she didn't like him. But the whole exchange just ruined everything she'd spent hours to accomplish. She placed the cupcake on the table in front of Zach's wheelchair. Suddenly, she didn't feel special anymore.

Chapter Four

KRISTA AWOKE AT four thirty for the early shift at work. It was already hot and humid, and the swamp coolers they had in each of their tiny rooms barely made a difference. The only thing they were good for was making puddles of muddy water on the outside of the windows they hung on. She was dressed and ready with fifteen minutes to spare. Walking out to the end of their old dock, she sat with her feet in the cool water of the marsh, sipping a cup of Earl Grey. The moon was full, and she watched the golden reflection dance on the still water. She wiggled her toes and appreciated the ripples it created. Simple cause and effect. She soaked in the peacefulness, in the sensation that time stood still.

A loud noise made her turn. The only other house on their bend of the marsh was almost a quarter mile away. The meticulously kept house belonged to Aunt Alice, who wasn't actually her aunt and who had passed on to the heavenly realm more than a year ago. Since then, Krista had heard rumors that Aunt Alice's adult kids might rent out the home, but it'd been quiet so far. She heard thuds and scuffling coming from the garden and pulled her feet out of the water. Overgrown roses blocked her view of the source of the noise coming from the perfect little off-white house at the end of a sparse forest. Just when she'd decided to walk over and check it out, she noticed a dark figure on Alice's dock. It was a man carrying what looked like a bucket. He reached the end, dipped the bucket into the water, set the filled container on the end of the dock, and walked away. A few minutes later, he was back with a ladder.

Who needed a ladder at the end of a boat dock?

Clearly, there was someone at Aunt Alice's, and from the look of the things, they were a bit odd. That was to be expected of marsh people. Krista tossed the rest of her lukewarm tea into the water and stood. So much for a peaceful morning.

Birdalee Mudge-Crane came to Tea and Tennyson early that day, and she was on a tear. "Where is Charlotte?" Birdie asked without a hello, her eagle eyes taking in every last person seated in a clear plastic chair in the modern black-and-white space.

"She's on the French Riviera. Her honeymoon," Krista reminded her.

Birdie grumbled as if Charlotte was supposed to still be living in her loft above the store, at Birdie's beck and call. "Why are all of my friends ignoring me?" she practically screamed. "I reckon if I was dying, y'all would pay me some attention. Do I have to die? Huh? Is that what I've got to do?" She stuck her neck out and widened her eyes like a cartoon character. "Cause I will, you know."

"Hey there, bitchy," Scruggs said, coming inside from the back patio, carrying his Yorkshire terrier named Waffles. Birdie turned on her favorite victim like an ax murderer.

"I smelled you before I saw you," she said, waving her hand in front of her nose. "You stop believing in showers?"

Scruggs put down Waffles and flipped his deep-parted, long bangs to the side when he stood back up. "How ya doin', ya big meanie?" Scruggs wasn't the tallest or most handsome college frat boy, but he had a way about him that made people want his attention. Maybe it was his sarcasm or his ability to laugh at himself. Whatever it was, Birdie reacted to it the opposite of everyone else.

"I'm worried. Not that you would care one bit," she said, pouting.

"About what?" He put on the same faux concerned face Birdie was wearing.

"Ginny."

Krista took the opportunity to get back to work.

"Aw. Is Virginia up to her old schemes again?" He practically sang the words.

"What the hell am I doing talking to you?" Birdie said. "Krista! Don't you dare walk away." She grabbed Krista by the hand and pulled her away from Scruggs, heading for her favorite seat by the window where everyone could see her. She talked the whole way.

"Now that Ginny's got herself some sort of fancy place out there in Charleston, she doesn't have time for her old friend Birdie anymore. Imagine not being able to spare one second for your childhood best friend," Birdie said, "for the person who has stood beside you through every mean and ridiculous thing you ever did. Hell, Virginia burned down her own house just to spite her stepdaughter, and who gave her a place to stay?" She slapped both her hands on the table causing everything except her immovable brown football helmet of hair to jiggle. "Me! That's who. Goddamn it. That woman is not allowed to ignore me." Before sitting, she snapped her fingers at Scruggs. "Go get me a cookie, screwy."

He gave her a thumbs-up that quickly switched to a middle finger.

"I saw Virginia at the Harris Teeter yesterday," Krista said.

Birdie turned to look at her so fast that her large dangling earring whacked her on the side of the face. "Ginny was at a grocery store? Which one? Ain't no Harris Teeter near here."

Krista nearly panicked. Why had she opened her mouth? Now she would have to explain why she'd driven all the way to North Charleston. There was no way she could tell the truth. "Zach had a doctor's appointment in West Ashley," she said. "I was just killing time." The acid in her stomach punished her for the lie. They couldn't afford any doctors that the state didn't pay for, and recently their only visits were free from hospice at their home.

Birdie appeared deep in thought. "Why in the hell was Ginny at a grocery store? And one so far away?"

"I got the sense that she wasn't shopping for herself. She was there with some man."

"Whaaa?" Birdie squawked. "You did *not* just say she was there with a man."

"I believe I did."

"What in the ever-loving—?" Birdie didn't finish her sentence because Scruggs had placed an iced oatmeal cookie in front of her. She took a large bite and practically swallowed it whole. "So, what did she say? You know, when you went up to her?"

"I didn't go up to her." Krista opted not to point out that she'd actually hidden from her.

"I knew you were going to say that." Birdie slammed the cookie on the table, crumbs flying in all directions. "Now, thanks to you and your lack of gumption, we have a genuine mystery on our hands."

Scruggs interjected, "You could always just ask her, you know."

"Don't go gettin' on my bad side, Scrooge. Ya hear?"

He chuckled. "Yes, ma'am."

"Well, if you do talk to her, please don't tell her that I was the one who said something," Krista said.

Birdie shot her a look. "I am nothing if not discreet."

Just as Scruggs burst into loud laughter, Krista noticed Johnny Merrick coming down the sidewalk toward the store.

"Shut your trap, Scrooby-doo," Birdie said. "Ooooh, here comes that fine-looking friend of Will's. You know, he asked my husband about you, Krista. Called him up special just to ask about the girl who took care of him at the wedding."

Well, that explained how he knew her name and place of business. Weren't pastors supposed to keep everything to themselves? Krista excused herself and headed toward the back patio as if she had important business to attend to. Hiding outside, she whispered to Waffles, who had his own posh doghouse in the corner, "Why is that man here again?" She straightened metal chairs and picked oak leaves off the ground. He hadn't even ordered anything last time, so it wasn't for the food. She heard the door open and felt someone watching her.

"You have to order up front," she said, knowing it was him without looking in his direction. "If you like chocolate, co-cola, and espresso, I recommend the Early Birdie Special."

"I figured you wouldn't call," he said. She slowly turned. Neither his face nor his voice held anger. It was simply a factual statement.

"Why on earth would I call you?" She put her handful of dead leaves in the tall trash can next to him.

"Do you live out by the marsh?" He leaned against the doorframe, casual and unbothered by her snipe. He was taller than her by at least a foot and was athletically built, but not in the same way as Rye. Where Rye was bulky and stout, Johnny was lean and cut. His T-shirt hugged his biceps, and his thighs pressed against the fabric of his jeans, but it was somehow not showy or even purposeful. With his short haircut, he looked like a soldier straight out of Hollywood.

She answered *yes* before she thought better of it. "I live with my mama and my little brother." She didn't want him to think she lived alone.

"I'm renting a place out there for the summer," he said. "I'm having a get-together for the Fourth of July this weekend, and I don't know many people out here. You're welcome to stop by. Bring whoever you want."

Her heart stopped. It was him she'd seen at the dock this morning. Him with the bucket and the ladder—for fireworks. It all made sense now. He was her neighbor for the summer? Was he stalking her? She should've felt frightened or at least threatened, but she didn't. What she did feel, however, was a strong certainty that she would not, under any circumstances, go to his party. And furthermore, she would make sure to avoid him all summer.

She was irked that he was inviting her to a get-together when he still hadn't apologized or said thank you, for that matter. That was the behavior of a narcissist. She may only have taken two online psychology courses through the community college so far, but she considered herself an expert in people. The disorder was more prevalent in men and involved an inflated sense of self-importance. She decided to test him. Narcissists didn't handle criticism well.

Pulling her shoulders back, she squared up, which caused him to stop leaning on the doorframe and tower in front of her. "Your card was unwelcome," she said. "Your phone number? I owe you one? If you had any manners at all, you woulda simply said the only two appropriate words for the situation: *I'm sorry.* Even a simple *thank-you* woulda been better than what I got."

"So, you didn't like my card."

She remembered the beautiful scene on the front and nearly answered differently. "No. I didn't like it."

"Okay, then." He stuffed his hands into his pockets, his dark hair framing the disappointed look on his face. "Well, I hope to see you on the Fourth. Come on over any time. We'll be in the back garden by the BBQ and out on the dock."

Krista turned away, her theory confirmed.

"Oh, and Krista?" he said. "Thank you for taking care of my drunk ass. I don't remember a whole lot about what I said at the wedding, but if I offended you, I'm truly sorry." His tone was actually contrite with a firm edge of genuine.

She felt called out. So, he may not be a narcissist, but he was definitely someone she needed to stay away from. She mumbled, "You're welcome," and left it at that.

Chapter Five

KRISTA SAT ON the dock near the water's edge with a bucket and two bags: one of powdered clay and the other of fish meal. She mixed them in a five-to-one ratio and added marsh water to form a paste. Then she made ten flat balls that resembled pizza dough and put each one on the dock to dry. It was a stinky job, and it always brought out the biting flies, but it had somehow become hers to do. Rye would be coming by in his fishing boat late that afternoon to pick them up. He had ten poles ready to bait and a size-seven cast net. He promised to bring them back a "big ole mess of them dadgum brown shrimp." He liked speaking like a redneck sometimes, as long as it wasn't around his mother. Brown shrimp were the summertime small shrimp, not the big, white ones that started growing in the fall, but all kinds of shrimp were good in a Lowcountry boil. Krista had the corn, the potatoes, the kielbasa sausage, and the enormous pot ready to go. Their Fourth of July was going to be delicious.

By the time the sky was orange-tinted, Krista, Junie, and Zach were all on the back porch waiting for Rye and his shrimp haul. Music filled the air from the party next door, and Krista adjusted the headrest on Zach's wheelchair so he could see the silhouettes of the partygoers milling around on the dock. Junie cracked open a cold beer. She did that all day long when the weather was hot. "Reckon someone took over Aunt Alice's place, huh?"

"Just a renter," Krista answered, fanning herself with an old advertisement. "Should be gone by the fall."

Thankfully, Junie accepted that answer. She didn't ask whether he was a man, if he had a wife, or how much money he made. Not that she even cared about the wife part. The whole town knew that Junie Hassell was on the prowl for a sugar daddy. Earl Hassell, Krista and Zach's father, had been gone for more than ten years, and not one person had heard a thing from him. No one blamed Junie, except maybe for the way she went about looking for his replacement. She used the old-school method: get drunk at a bar, show too much skin, and go home with whoever paid you the most attention. Junie still had a little bloom on her, and from far away she was downright pretty. But her sagging jowls, graying hair, and hot pink painted lips told a different story up close. Krista knew all about what her mother did, not just because she'd had to pick her up at three A.M. or wake her up at three P.M., but also because she'd cleaned the vomit from the floor and wiped the mascara from beneath her mother's bloodshot eyes. Plus, the woman had no verbal filter when she was drunk.

Krista stood to turn on the porch lights. She'd already fed Zach through his tube, and the water was boiling on the stove, ready to dump in the ingredients. She listened to the cicadas while she waited, her stomach growling.

"Krista!" came a voice from down the way. "Is that you?" One of the silhouettes from next door had walked halfway to her house and was waving. It was a female voice, but Charlotte was on her honeymoon. Who else would be invited to Will's friend's party?

"Hey, sweetheart! It's Ruth Marie!"

The shadowy figure picked up the pace and jogged toward Krista. Ruth Marie was always the same—not a hair out of place in her chic blonde bob, makeup applied like a professional, clothing perfectly tailored and on-trend, and even her fingernails were never too long, uneven, or unpainted. Krista had to fight off the wave of embarrassment that always threatened her confidence whenever someone saw the way she lived, but with Ruth Marie, it was a tidal wave. It wasn't Krista's fault that she lived in a hovel. She'd left her own apartment and a great job in Myrtle Beach to come back and help her little brother. Family had to come first, and anyone with morals and values would appreciate that. She took a deep breath, opened the ratty screen door, and walked down the back steps toward the figure.

"Hey, Ruth Marie!" Krista ran, trying to keep her as far away as possible from the house. Both girls hugged. Ruth Marie was Charlotte's sister-in-law and thereby one of the nice ones.

"Why aren't you at the party? Johnny said he invited you." There wasn't reproach in her voice, just what seemed to be a true desire to have Krista there.

"Mama, Zachy, and I are waiting for Rye to get back with a mess of shrimp. We're having ourselves a boil tonight."

"Mmmm. Well, you ought to come on by afterward. Jack and I got a babysitter for Lauren, so we are partying it up tonight!"

Krista laughed. Ruth Marie's idea of partying it up was one glass of Sauvignon Blanc and half a bite of a cupcake. "I wish I could," she said. "But with Rye coming by and all..."

"Hey, over there!" came a voice from near the dock. Krista assumed it was Jack coming to make nice since she was in conversation with his wife. Krista wished she was wearing something other than old cutoff jean shorts and a tank top. Jack was a Buchanan, Virginia's son, and even though he had always been nice to her, the Buchanans were the cream of Crickley Creek's crop. They were quick to remind people of that fact, too.

As the figure drew closer, Krista's heart seized. It was Johnny, running full speed toward her. "Hey! Krista!" He stopped in front of her, his face glowing in the setting sun. "Here." He handed her a bunch of unlit sparklers like they were flowers.

She took them. "Thank you."

"You ever held a sparkler before?" He smiled as if there was nothing weird between them.

"I wasn't raised on the moon," she answered. "I've held a sparkler before."

Ruth Marie laughed before turning serious again. "How's Zach doing?"

"Aw, you know," Krista said. "He's twenty-one now."

Anyone who knew about Duchenne muscular dystrophy understood that many of them didn't survive past their teens. "I'm sorry, honey." Ruth Marie hugged Krista while Johnny looked on.

Krista acted like the hug was a goodbye. When she pulled away, she said, "Thanks for stopping by y'all. Have a great time at the party!" And she turned and walked back to her house, hoping Ruth Marie didn't feel like she'd been short with her. Johnny could feel whatever damn way he wanted to. He was a visitor to Crickley and would not amount to anything.

Krista and Junie had the sparklers shooting glitter fire by the time Rye pulled up in his camouflage fishing boat. They wrote words in the air with the glow of the stick. Zach giggled and soaked in the white light of the sparks against the black sky. Krista wrote out *Kiki loves Zachy* as Rye, carrying an ice chest, walked up the patchy grass lawn. Behind him, colorful splashes erupted from all over the marsh—off of hidden boats and over the treetops from the beach on the other side. But they were all eclipsed by the show next door, where they not only shot off the big ones, they blasted patriotic songs by Neil Diamond and Lee Greenwood and Bruce Springsteen, like a proper Independence Day celebration. The sound floated with the humidity through the hot air.

For not having many friends in the area, Johnny Merrick had drawn a crowd. Krista watched the silhouetted figures move around, like apparitions floating over the marsh. Some people sat with their feet dangling over the side of the dock, cooling in the water, and others laughed and danced around so quickly, it was hard to keep track of them. She imagined herself at the party, dressed up and smiling, chatting comfortably with Ruth Marie and Jack and whoever else stood at the end of Johnny's dock.

In her daydream, she was happy and confident, moving from group to group, cracking jokes and giving compliments. She was welcomed, and it wasn't because she was pretty. No, the feeling she had was deeper, richer, more long-lasting. It was the feeling of fitting in, of belonging with the mix of people on that dock, being of like mind, and having something to offer—humor, compassion, intelligence, or at least something in common. For a moment, the restlessness that had been niggling at her like a rock in her shoe was gone, and the stomach-burning regret of having to say no to Johnny's invitation had been replaced by happiness. She felt the peace she desperately craved. When she realized she was smiling toward the crowd, the sweet dream, and her happiness, snapped like a stepped-on twig as reality hit her—her falling-apart home, donated sparklers, and Rye Smithson trudging up her lawn, dripping with sweat and frowning.

"Who in the hell are those people?" he asked when Krista opened the screen door for him. He trudged in and slammed down the bucket. "Did they give y'all those sparklers?"

"Nope. Don't know 'em." Krista hoped he couldn't see her face in the dark.

Chapter Six

SCRUGGS SHOWED UP to work with a long, white mystery box tied with a pink bow. Roses, Krista presumed. She knew immediately who they were for. Poor little Emma was about to get the full balls-to-the-wall romantic treatment from ol' Scruggs.

He should never have worn his light pink polo shirt. Not only were the sweat rings under his arms a contrasting dark pink, but his cheeks looked like he'd just put on his mother's old Mary Kay Shy Blush rouge. The man was as rosy as Aunt Alice's garden in the summertime.

Emma was in the back kitchen, pulling pastries from the refrigerator to put in the display, while Scruggs walked back and forth in front of the counter, pacing like a zoo-ed up lion. He had just a few minutes before they had to unlock the doors for customers, so he'd better hurry. He threw his keys onto the counter, clearly hoping that the noise would bring Emma from the kitchen. Was he shaking? He was shaking. Krista tried not to laugh. She twisted her long, blonde hair into a knot on her head and pretended not to be watching the scene unfold.

Emma walked out of the kitchen, carrying a tray. She didn't even glance at Scruggs, just went to work placing the pastries on their assigned dishes.

He walked with a purpose around the counter. "Well, hey there, Miss Emma," he said, his voice sounding three octaves lower than normal. "I, uh, brought you a little somethin'."

When Emma turned to look at him, Krista liked to have fainted clean away. The girl had love in her eyes. Or the possibility of it, at least. What on earth was happening?

She took the box like it was filled with rare and highly breakable glass, set it on the counter, and opened it. Then she pulled out the most interesting mix of flowers Krista ever saw. She stopped pretending not to watch so she could get a closer look. Surely, her own face mirrored Emma's surprise.

"They're made out of Legos," Emma said, her eyes wide.

"I made them," Scruggs replied, quite pleased with himself.

Never before, without stepping on them first, had Krista seen Legos make a woman cry. Yet there was Emma, bawling her eyes out like Scruggs Willingham III had just proposed marriage.

Scruggs went from pink and nervous back to king of the world in 2.2 seconds. *Who would have guessed it?* thought Krista as the two embraced. She moved to unlock the front door, barely looking outside before she turned the key. A tall woman in a cream-colored pantsuit walked through the door and caught her by surprise.

"Good morning, Krista," Virginia said.

"Good morning, Ms. Buchanan. Come on in! We have a peach tart on special today if you're interested." Krista tried to sound cheery as she walked away.

"May I have a word with you?"

Krista stopped dead in her tracks. *Oh, no.* "Of course," she replied, following Virginia to a nearby table. She pulled a face at Scruggs and Emma, who had just taken notice of her predicament.

"Now, it has come to my attention that your brother is seeing a doctor in West Ashley," Virginia began.

Krista's face heated as she sat down. She had to think quickly to cover her lie. "Well, that was just a one-time visit."

"May I ask which physician he saw?"

"Umm, I don't remember the name. Maybe Shar-Pei? Or something." Crap. She panicked.

Virginia said nothing, just stared at her. "Like the breed of dog?"

"Well, like I said, I don't really remember." Krista moved to stand.

"Have yourself a seat, dear."

She slowly sat back down, noticing that a line was forming at the counter and she should be there to help.

"Correct me if I'm wrong, but it's beginning to appear as if you weren't supposed to be out that way." Virginia had a malevolent stare that somehow made her eyes look light purple and scarily inhuman.

"Last I checked," Krista said, "I can go wherever I want." Time stopped in that moment. Krista sat straight up to fully face her attacker. Movement through the window behind Virginia caught her eye. It was a tall man in board shorts and a plain navy T-shirt: Johnny. She prayed he would keep walking and not come into the store. Why was he coming by every flippin' day?

"I know exactly what you were doing all the way out in North Charleston all by yourself." Virginia smirked. "Like mother, like daughter."

The front door opened, and Johnny walked in. Krista ignored him, still slack-jawed with awe that Virginia could be so blatantly mean. She'd thrown down the gauntlet. Krista didn't have time to formulate a response before Virginia raised her voice loud enough for the entire store to hear.

"Clearly, you were meeting a man. And I'm certain it was not your boyfriend, Rye Smithson." Virginia gracefully stood from her chair like the victor in a duel. "I saw you," she said. "And if you deny it, it will only serve to prove my point." The hideous woman scooted out her chair, shot a disgusted look around the room, and sashayed away.

"I was not!" Krista had the intense desire to throw something at her as she exited the store.

As if the curiosity on Scruggs's and Emma's faces wasn't

enough, Johnny Merrick's look of entertainment—he'd been standing just inside the front door during the scene—sent her over the edge. "I hate that woman!" Krista breathed, her fists clenched. "I was not meeting a man," she said louder. "I would never do that."

"That woman is worse than a cottonmouth," Scruggs said, coming to her rescue.

Emma nodded.

"I know what she's doing," Krista said to anyone who was listening.

Johnny, who was in line behind a woman wearing overalls, commented, "Looked like she was poking the bear to me."

Krista eyed him with disdain. "If you were from here, you'd know better." The small dig made her feel the tiniest bit mollified. "It wasn't about me at all. It was completely about her."

The woman in overalls said, "Amen."

"Deny everything and immediately make counter-accusations. That's what we do here," Krista said. "She was accusing me of what she was caught doing. It's called deflection."

The woman in overalls nodded vigorously. "So that's what they call it." She pulled out her phone and began typing in the word.

Scruggs still looked confused.

"See, when the gossipers start talking about Virginia being seen in North Charleston with a man, she can say, *Oh, no, you've got that backward. Krista Hassell didn't catch me, I caught Krista Hassell.* And plenty of people will believe her because so-and-so heard her accuse me at the coffee shop."

Johnny's eyebrows were raised. "That's a damn good strategy."

Scruggs hissed and pretended two of his fingers were snake fangs.

Emma was actively taking coffee orders, her plastic flowers safely in the back room. "I'm not saying anyone will talk to me about this, but I will absolutely back you up if they do," she said. "You would never cheat on Rye. Or anyone. We know this. Don't you worry."

"Thanks, Emma." Krista noted that, despite her frustration, at least Johnny now knew she had a boyfriend.

"Me, too," Scruggs said. The entire rest of the room agreed.

"So, what is the truth again?" Emma asked. "You were there for your brother's doctor's appointment?"

Krista nodded.

She'd never get away from her own lie.

Chapter Seven

After her morning shift, Krista took another tiny Charleston Blush Noisette rosebush she and Zach had propagated from cuttings years ago. Every time they went to the beach house, they dug one up from their garden and added it to Charlotte and Will's, knowing that one day, Zach would be remembered by those flowers. He had a hand in making their favorite place even more beautiful. It was a small price to pay for leaving a legacy. At home, over the years, Zach also planted bulbs. That way, when the ranunculus, lilies, and dahlias emerged from the ground, it would be like he was coming back to say hello.

A pop-up thunderstorm had just quelled, so when Krista pulled up to the beach house, the ground was wet and steamy. She pulled Zach's wheelchair from her trunk and locked it in position beside the open passenger door. Then the hard part, lifting him. He could no longer hold on to her neck, so she had to get under his armpits and lift him carefully. She was dripping with sweat by the time he was safely seated. "Okay, buddy. Let's go." She pushed the chair along the gravel path to the back door where Will had built a ramp. Before they went up, Krista locked his wheels in place and ran to the shed for a shovel. "Does this spot look good?"

Zach answered slowly, "Perfect."

Krista dug a hole in a spot by the house that would get plenty of sun, slipped in the tiny rosebush and covered it back up. "Done."

"Hey, Kiki?"

"Yeah, bud?"

He strained to enunciate each quietly spoken word. "When I die, will you sprinkle my ashes in our garden?"

Her breath caught in her throat. "Of course."

"And, Kiki?"

"Yeah?"

"Would you save some? A long time from now when you die, can you have someone put some of my ashes with yours?"

She shook from the effort of suppressing the deep blow of sorrow. "Absolutely."

"Thanks," he said.

She walked over and kissed his cheek, holding her muddy hands away from him. "Let me just go wash my hands and we'll head inside." She was using the hose to get the mud from underneath her fingernails when she heard a thud. Her head flew around to Zach, who was sprawled out on the ground. As she ran to him, she could tell exactly what happened. His right wheel sank in the soft earth, and when his body weight shifted, the chair fell sideways. "Zachy!" She lifted his limp head, which had a contusion on the side. "Zachy! I'm so sorry!"

"I'm okay," he said as she cradled his head in her lap.

"Shit! How am I going to get you up?" Getting him from the car was one thing, but trying to lift him from the ground was another. "Help!" she yelled, feeling as ridiculous as she felt helpless. Chances were slim that anyone else was within hearing distance. "Help!"

No one showed, of course. Like a metaphor for her life, she would have to figure out how to solve the problem alone.

She held Zachy's head in her lap.

"I'm okay," he said.

"How about your arm?" she asked. "You probably fell pretty hard onto it, and your shoulder."

"They're fine."

"I'm so sorry," she kept saying.

She unbuckled Zach from his chair and gently laid him on the ground as she set the chair upright, brushing the mud from the armrest. Krista was used to Zach being helpless; she'd been witness to his slow decline. But the finality of it hit her in that moment. First, he couldn't walk, then he couldn't feed himself, and now… now he was completely reliant on her and Junie to keep him alive when what he truly deserved was to have the longest, happiest life.

"All right, your turn, bud."

With all her might, she tenderly lifted him from the ground, his head slumped onto her shoulder. He was taller than her, so getting his rear onto the seat seemed impossible. Yet somehow they managed. She set his emaciated body in the chair, scooted him backward, leaned his head into the headrest and buckled him in. Once he was settled, she pushed him carefully up the ramp. At the top, she tilted the blue-and-white ceramic pot to retrieve the key hidden underneath and swung open the French doors into the kitchen. Once inside, she went straight to the sink and wet paper towels to clean him off. There was no way to hold back the tears as she wiped his withered arms.

"I'm okay, Kiki."

"Thank God." She kissed him again on the cheek she'd just cleaned. "I can't live without you."

"You're gonna have to," he whispered.

Krista knew he was right. And it was going to be soon.

They watched the sunset from the front porch. It was different than the marsh.

There was sand, for one, and the grasses weren't as green or plentiful. A squadron of pelicans flew overhead, and seagulls cried out their endless hunger. Standing in the distance on top of a dune was a bobcat—easy to identify by his stubbed tail. But their favorite thing to watch were the fireflies. It was a game to see who would spot the first one. Sometimes a moth in a light would trick them, and other times there was one flash, never to be seen again. But on a good night, they'd be plentiful, hovering in the dark between the trees like lantern fairies, with crickets playing violins for their dance. Something about them was quintessentially Southern, and when she got lost in their light display, she actually felt proud to live in a place like Crickley Creek.

Zach saw the first tail light up that night. "I'm the lucky one," he announced.

But Krista knew the truth. She was the lucky one. Lucky to have someone like Zach for a brother, lucky to have a home, a job, and a family. Lucky to have friends.

She was going to need them.

Chapter Eight

BIRDIE FLEW INTO Tea and Tennyson like a songbird in a windstorm. "Ooooo-eeeeeee. I tell you what," she said, dumping her large red purse on the closest table. "Just when I thought the woman had changed her colors, she's right back to doing what she does best: ruining lives."

Krista knew exactly who Birdie was talking about. And exactly whose life was being ruined.

"Krista, we need to have us a sit-down." She pointed to the seat beside her. "Now."

Krista looked over to Emma, who mouthed "go" and shooed her away. The morning rush was over, so it should be fine if Emma ran the register and made the drinks for a few minutes.

"Honey, Virginia is spreading so much hooey about you right now, I can't even keep up." She reached out and patted Krista's ice-cold hand. "Of course, I know that your version is the truth. If we can just figure out who Virginia was with that day in North Charleston, we would have ourselves some ammunition to fight back."

"I wish I knew. I've never seen him before."

"Well, I had me an idea. Lookie here." Birdie pulled out her phone. "It took me some doing, but I spent hours on the Google last night pulling up pictures of all of the single wealthy men of a certain age in North Charleston. Now, take a look at these and tell me if you recognize any of 'em."

Birdie might be on to something. Krista flipped through at least ten men. Not one looked familiar.

"Dadgummit," Birdie said. "Okay, then. Plan B. We're gonna have to get that doctor that Zach was seeing to make an appearance out here and prove he exists. He's got to come into the store and verify your story. Does the man make house calls to bookstores?"

Krista shuddered. "Birdie. We cannot afford a house call."

"Well, dammit all to hell." Birdie threw her phone into her purse and spent some time straining herself by thinking. "It looks like you're screwed, dear heart."

If only Birdie knew the full extent.

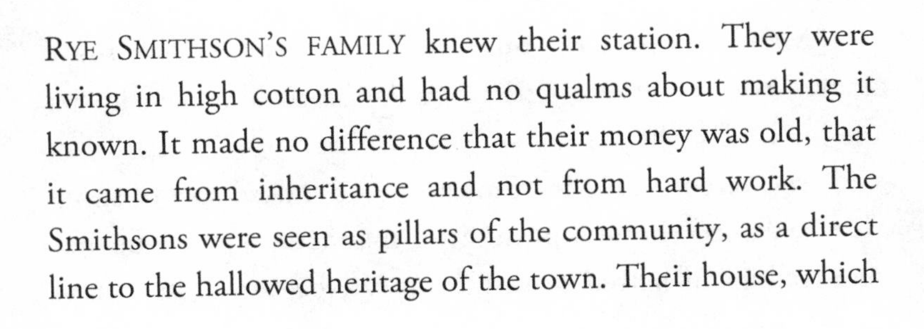

RYE SMITHSON'S FAMILY knew their station. They were living in high cotton and had no qualms about making it known. It made no difference that their money was old, that it came from inheritance and not from hard work. The Smithsons were seen as pillars of the community, as a direct line to the hallowed heritage of the town. Their house, which was referred to as Smithson House, exemplified them perfectly. It was octagonal, a fad dating back to the mid-1800s. The woodwork was lace-like and Victorian, but what set the house apart from any other home in the area was the domed cupola as high and ostentatious as the dome topping the nation's capitol building. It was like a fancy cherry on top of a strange antique that everyone admired but no one really wanted.

Krista was expected to bring a hostess gift. It was not often that she was invited to join Rye's family for a meal. It had taken years just to be allowed on their property. She used her employee discount to buy the newest coffee table book from *Architectural Digest*. It was thick and heavy with a hardcover that felt like cloth. The title was foil stamped, and the colors were neutral and wouldn't clash with all of the interior burgundies and forest greens of Smithson House. There was no more expensive book to be found in town. Rye's mother was going to love it. It was just like the woman herself—neutral on the outside, but filled with strong opinions and a lust for opulence and superiority on the inside.

"Mama," Rye said, pushing Krista through the front door. "You remember Krista." As if she hadn't been in his life for a full eight years.

"Yes, of course." Mrs. Smithson had a dead sort of smile that screamed she was putting on manners to cover up her real feelings of hatred or disgust or, at the very least, disappointment. "Welcome back, dear."

The dinner table was set with real china and cloth napkins. The Hassells might've been white trash, but Junie did know her manners, and she taught them to her children. Krista put her napkin on her lap, and once the meal was served, waited for Mrs. Smithson to pick up her fork before lifting her own. There was very little conversation. Mr. Smithson sat like Abraham Lincoln, tall and stiff, at the head of the table.

"This salad is delicious," Krista said, making sure she was using the shorter fork on the outside of the setting.

"If you like beets," Mrs. Smithson replied. "I will tell Sharon to leave them out next time."

Rye reached over and squeezed her hand underneath the table. At least he was aware of how difficult his parents were. She smiled her gratitude at him.

"So, Krista. How is that mother of yours doing?" Mrs. Smithson asked. "Bless her heart, it must be so hard for her, with your brother being the way he is and no husband around to be of help." Her smile was less dead that time. The sneaky mockery was giving her a glow.

"She's good. Thanks." Krista felt like she needed to add something more in order to be friendlier, but Junie didn't have a job, she didn't volunteer anywhere—she just took care of Zach and snuck out to God-only-knew where every night. "Mama has taken up knitting. She's been making caps that she plans to donate for babies at hospitals." It was only a partial lie. Junie had taken up knitting, but the caps part of the story came straight from something Krista had once seen on the news. Junie didn't have that kind of follow-through, or money for yarn.

For the first time, Mr. Smithson spoke up. "Caps for babies? Seems like there ought to be a better use of her time. There are jobs to be had. She could work at the McDonalds or be one of those greeters at the Wal-Mart. Make herself a useful part of society."

Heat rose in Krista's face as she bit her tongue. Who would take care of Zach if her mother wasn't home? Plus, her mother worked hard, and had more compassion in her little toe than this whole family had for a hundred years back. Not to mention, all that man did was golf and manage his investments. He'd never held a real job in his life. He wasn't one to talk.

Krista took a bite of buttered roll, then found Rye's hand and squeezed again, hard. *Please, God,* she thought. *I will never tell another lie if you just end this dinner soon.*

When she was finally back in Rye's truck, she felt like bruises and scratches should be evident all over her body. She'd just taken an emotional beating.

"Man, that cake was good," Rye said. "I don't know how Sharon makes the cake layers so thin with all that caramel in between like that. My belly thanks her." He patted what used to be a flat, toned abdomen but had in the past couple of years expanded to a much rounder shape.

"It was good," she said, not actually remembering anything aside from her desperate desire to escape. Every time she was around Rye's parents, she was reminded of what her mother once said about not marrying just the man but the whole family. It was going to take a lot to learn to love the Smithsons. But her children wouldn't have the worries that she did. Her children would have a better life. As Junie always said, "I could stand on my head in a bucket of shit if it meant I could provide for my family." Of course, Junie said it but never did it. Krista would be different.

Krista would actually do it.

Chapter Nine

THE NOON SHIFT meant sleeping in. It was one of the small pleasures Krista tried to fully appreciate. Junie was home to take care of Zach, so when he was up and out, she moved to the middle of the bed and spread out like a starfish. The house wasn't too hot for the sheets yet.

An hour later, she padded into the kitchen like a lazy cat, ready for a cup of tea and a chat with her family. She hadn't even bothered to brush her teeth, just pulled out a chair and plopped into it.

"There you are!" came her mother's voice from the back porch. "Come on out here. We're having ourselves a friendly visit with our neighbor."

Krista quickly stuffed the cold remnants of Junie's biscuit breakfast into her mouth to combat what was surely rancid breath, then shuffled her way outside.

"Hey!" Johnny said. "Love the pajamas."

They were rainbow, and what used to be full-length pants were now capris. He'd probably been up since dawn, run ten miles, taken a shower, and now stood confidently in his brand-name outfit. He was brazen enough to act like he fit in at her place as well as he would fit in anywhere else—like the freaking Academy Awards or Harvard. He was too outgoing, too citified, and too damned confident. And, of course, he'd caught her looking like she just walked out of an episode of the People of Walmart. Her skin burned with embarrassment and irritation. She shot him her most disdainful look.

"So, I have to go back to Chicago for a bit," he said. "Mostly, I can run my business from out here, but every now and then I have to get back to the office."

Was he bragging? He had some sort of fancy job that required him to go into an office in Chicago? Krista made sure her face showed a distinct lack of appreciation for his boast.

Junie, who had been watching her and frowning, clapped her hands together as if his statement deserved applause. "That is so exciting! Yes, yes. You must get back to Chicago—as long as you promise to come right back here to us. Ya hear me?"

"I will," he said. "Would you mind keeping an eye on the house while I'm gone? I promised my landlords that I would take care of it, and I don't know how long I'll be away. I'll leave my cell phone number with you in case anything comes up."

"Of course, of course," Junie said. "We would absolutely love to." You'd have thought she was being asked to house sit a food-filled air-conditioned mansion.

Johnny turned his gaze to Krista. "Will you miss me?"

What kind of obnoxious question was that? He knew she had a boyfriend. "How would I miss someone I never think about? Someone who means absolutely nothing to me."

Junie reached over and slapped her hard on the arm.

"Ow! Mother!"

"Where are your manners?" she chided. "We all like you very much, Johnny Merrick." She spoke his name in a way that sounded reverent, like he was a movie star or the president.

Krista cringed, then sweetly offered up, "We would be very happy to watch Aunt Alice's house. Like we always do." Then she ended it with, "Take your time in Chicago."

Johnny acted like he didn't hear her. "Great! Krista, could I get you to follow me over to the house? I'll show you where the hidden key is."

"You can just tell me where it is," she said, pointing to her bare feet.

"Not a problem." He started toward her, making it clear that he was about to carry her.

"Don't you touch me!" She jumped back. The audacity of that man. He thought he was hilarious, but he was really just a jerk. "You will wait until I put my shoes on." Like she was the princess of a castle and not the inhabitant of a barely standing shack, she proudly went inside. Taking her time, she changed into a pair of jean shorts and a pink tank top, then brushed her sleep-messed hair into a ponytail and slipped on her flip-flops. She even brushed her teeth. Johnny was chatting it up with Junie on the sofa when she reappeared.

He led the way to his house with legs that were so long, she had to walk double-time to keep up with him. "You might ought to slow down," she said. "It's snake season."

If anything, his pace increased. When they got to Aunt Alice's house, she was a little out of breath. He pulled the key from under the mat. "I might as well just give this to you," he said.

She took the key and turned to leave. "You coulda just dropped this off and saved me the trouble." He clearly enjoyed pulling her out of her comfort zone.

"Hey, Krista?" he ventured.

She turned back around.

"Can I ask you a question?"

"I don't know, can you?" She was being sassy, and it sure felt good.

"What do you want most in the world?" He leaned against the door like it was a casual question he regularly asked people.

"I'm trying to leave here." She took one step down the stairs.

"I can see that. Please, just one little question."

"One very personal question." She was sure he was trying to get her to talk about her boyfriend. He was probably expecting her to say that all she wanted in the world was to get married, to have a man rescue her from her sorry life.

"Yes, that's the point." He was still smiling. She could shoot that man with verbal bullets all day and he wouldn't succumb.

She knew the answer immediately, but she didn't want to talk about it. Didn't want to think about it. It was none of his business. She battled between her annoyance and her desire to give him an answer he didn't expect. In the end, it was an opportunity to show him that she wasn't the shallow little small-town girl he thought she was.

"There are two things I want," she said finally. "I want my brother to be whole and healthy again. And I want to get the hell out of Crickley Creek."

She didn't ask him the question back, and she didn't stay for his reaction. Instead, she bolted back to her house like her hair was on fire. She couldn't let him see the ambush emotions that took her over the moment she spoke the words. Sometimes the power of the truth hit like a sledgehammer.

THAT AFTERNOON, RYE came into the store. Rye never visited Krista at work. He looked upon her job as he would look upon wearing seersucker or the color pink—something for Charleston sissies. But here he was, standing in the corner by the fiction section, waiting for Krista to take a break. She knew she was in trouble by the set of his jaw. The rumor

Virginia had been spreading must've gotten to him. If Krista had been smart, she would have told him everything right when it was happening. With his family part of high society, she hadn't wanted him to know that she was on Virginia Buchanan's bad side. It was enough already that she was a Hassell. Now it was too late. She kicked herself for not wanting to rock the boat.

As soon as she could take her ten-minute break, she walked over to him. "Hey," she said.

"We're not doing this here," he replied, quickly turning toward the front door so that she had to follow him like a child. "Get in," he said when they got to his Hummer, not bothering to open the door for her.

He started the engine.

"I can't go anywhere. I'm still working," she said.

"Well, is it all right with you if I have myself some air-conditioning while sittin' in my own vehicle?" It was more of a snarky remark than a question.

"Of course," she said sweetly.

"First of all," he said, turning his whole body toward her and holding up his pointer finger. "You flirted with another man at the wedding. You can't deny it. I saw the card."

"No, I didn't—"

"Let me finish," Rye interrupted. "That was strike one." With his pointer finger still up, he added his middle finger. "Two. You had sparklers you said no one gave you. But I know damned well you wouldn't spend the money on something like that. I saw them next door twirling them things around. You lied to me, and I do not stand for lies."

Krista sat quietly, her heart racing. She couldn't lose Rye. Ever since she was forced to give up her job in Myrtle Beach, he'd been her future. He was all she had.

"Now, here's the thing," he said. "I believe in the *three strikes you're out* rule. If you mess up once, shame on you. If you mess up twice, it might be a coincidence. But if you mess up three times, that there's a pattern. That's when it becomes shame on me for stayin'."

Krista braced herself.

"Three." He added his ring finger and put all three in front of her face. "I hear from none other than my old friend Bucky that you drove all the way out to North Charleston to meet some guy. Virginia Buchanan saw you sitting at a bar." He was so furious, he could barely speak. "With your hand on some dude's knee."

"What?!" Krista nearly popped. She shouldn't have been surprised. That's what happened with rumors—grocery stores turned into bars. "That is a lie. I saw *her*. I saw Virginia with a man, but not at a bar. It was at the Harris Teeter."

He pushed a *you're a liar* puff of air from his nose. "Let's just pretend for a second that you're telling the truth. Then what in the hell were you doing at the Harris Teeter all the way out there?"

Krista recognized the moment of truth. She had to tell him. "Please don't judge me for what I'm about to say, okay?"

He didn't answer, just glared at her with his lips in a straight-across line and his eyes burning with fire.

"For a while now, when I'm not feeling happy or things aren't going too good, I get all dressed up and treat myself to something at the grocery store." She took a deep breath. "I don't go here in Crickley Creek, because it's not the same. I have to go somewhere that people don't know me."

Rye squinted suspiciously.

"I bought Zach a cupcake, you remember? You were there when I got home with it. But that wasn't why I went." She took a deep breath. Her secret was about to be out. "It was for the compliments. See, when I'm feeling low, it helps me to get compliments from strangers. I feel like a real person. Like I can be anyone. Like for a minute, I don't have to be Krista Hassell from Crickley Creek. Plus, a grocery store is a safe place. Do you see what I'm saying?"

His face was all screwed up and distorted like he had just discovered that she was certifiably insane.

"It's a little thing I do to make myself feel better," she said. "I guess I kinda feel noticed that way."

"You expect me to believe that?"

"Well, I've been thinking a lot about why I do it. I think, you know, with my family and all, that the one thing I have that sets me apart is the way I look. Mama put me in all of those beauty pageants growing up. And I remember being just fourteen and Junie wouldn't let me out of the house without a full face of makeup on. I know that was wrong of her, but I felt important in those days. Like that was the only reason she loved me."

"So, you're telling me that you go to grocery stores in North Charleston so that men will tell you you're pretty."

"Not men. Just anyone." She felt like a reprimanded three-year-old. "I don't care who notices me. It just matters that someone does."

"Right. Like I'm supposed to believe that you get all dolled up for some old lady in the bread aisle to tell you that you're pretty."

It sounded ridiculously stupid.

"Do I look like I just fell off the goddamn turnip truck?" He was getting louder. "Even if that was what you were doing, you lied to me again. You said you were running errands for the store." His fingers were in her face again. "I have given you eight years of my life, Krista. Eight *years.* And I dated your sorry ass even though your family made me look like I was slumming. I threw you a lifeline and this is how you repay me?"

"I have never gone anywhere to pick up men. I have never cheated on you."

"Three strikes, baby." He nearly poked her in the eyes with his three fingers. "You're out."

Krista was too stunned to move.

"My family never liked you anyway." Rye reached across and opened her door from the inside. "Now, get the hell out of my truck."

Even though her heart was in her throat and her blood ran like acid at the injustice, she did as she was told.

Chapter Ten

THE HOUSE PHONE rang at two A.M. Krista rolled over to check Zach's breathing as she did several times a night, then threw off the covers and ran to the kitchen where the yellowing spiral-corded phone hung on the wall. She'd been awake anyway, her head and heart still reeling over everything Rye had said when he broke up with her. There had to be a way to make things better.

She stubbed her toe on an uplifted piece of wood flooring just before she answered with a pained, "Hello?"

"Come get your mother—she's boutta get herself hurt."

Shit. "Where is she?"

The deep-voiced, thick-accented man answered, "She's at the end of the old fishing pier off the highway to Charleston."

Krista didn't even bother asking who he was. She hung up the phone, knowing exactly where he was talking about. It was a spot on the Ashley River, the best place to hunt for shark teeth, aside from inland creeks and construction sites where the megalodons were found. But Junie wasn't there to hunt for teeth, of course. Junie was there because it was an empty, hidden space and she was drunk out of her mind. Again.

Krista told Zach where she was going, then sped toward the highway. She pulled off on the side road just before the bridge and didn't bother with the parking spaces. Screeching to a stop at the pier, she threw open her door. "Mama!"

The sound of tires on gravel alerted her to a pickup truck leaving. It was probably whoever had called her, whoever had taken Junie to a private spot for God-only-knew what.

"Mama! Get down from there!" Junie was perched precariously on the rotting wooden railing, way out at the end, in the depths where the big fish lurked underneath. Krista ran along the splintering dock. The nearer she got, the drunker her mother appeared. "Don't move, Mama. I'm coming." It felt like the pier was a mile long as her mother teetered on the edge. "Don't move!"

She grabbed Junie around the waist, pulling her backward off the railing, her long exposed breasts hanging to one side. Junie muttered and spat, but it was all incomprehensible. "Shhhh, Mama. Let's just get you to the car."

By the time they got to her little blue Mustang, Krista had sweat through her pajamas. For a little thing, Junie was hard to drag. She was now slumped in the passenger seat, buckled—thanks to great strain on Krista's part—and drooling.

It had been two months since Junie's last episode, so Krista should've known it was coming. She'd done a lot of research about acting out. When Zach could still move, Junie was actually a pretty good mother, except for her bad temper and refusal to get a job. Zach was her job, she'd said.

But for the past several years since Zach couldn't move his arms, all of Junie's feelings started coming out sideways. She was anticipating Zach's death, and the grief was overwhelming her. It was understandable, really. Krista was living in dread, too. That's why she was back home. That's why she left the best job she'd ever had—the one that had finally gotten her out of Crickley Creek. The one that allowed her to feel like a valuable person instead of someone to be made fun of, looked down upon, and even despised. She knew how Junie felt because she loved Zach, too, and because they shared a last name—Hassell.

She understood perfectly why Junie was drinking.

After less than two hours of sleep, Krista called in sick to work. Scruggs and Emma probably wouldn't mind being alone in the store together anyway. She had to take care of Zach while Junie slept off the brown bottle flu. And Krista could use a little time, too. Despite the sunshine and blue skies over the marsh, she was exhausted and embarrassed, again, for her family. Plus, she was missing Rye something awful. Maybe if she just saw him, if she went over to his house and explained about the wedding and the sparklers, if she humbled herself more about the grocery store compliments, maybe he would forgive her.

With a little luck and enough food and water, by that

evening, Junie might be well enough for her to leave. Krista monitored her mother all day, checking for signs that she was capable again, but Junie appeared to be milking the fact that Krista was temporarily at her beck and call. By late afternoon, when the house was hotter than the swamp coolers could chill and they all had to sit out on the back porch for the breeze and the ceiling fans, it was clear that Junie had recovered. She had a big wad of chaw in her mouth that she spat with precision into a tall plastic cup.

"I'm going over to Rye's," Krista said, heading back inside. "See y'all later." Her mother had no idea that Rye had recently dumped her.

Junie raised a hand of farewell and continued rocking back and forth in her grandma's old wooden chair because the sofa was too hot on days like this. Zach was stationed next to her in his wheelchair, a wet cooling towel around his neck.

She texted Rye when she got in the car. *"You home?"* He didn't answer, but he was most likely either at his hunting lodge or Smithson House. She'd start with the hunting lodge first.

The shiny, brand-new cabin was lit up like a warning to any animal that might draw near. Danger: Men with guns inside. Rye's Hummer wasn't on the driveway, but she rang the doorbell just in case he'd parked it in the garage. No one answered. She rang again, listening for any sound coming from inside. There was nothing.

She knew what she had to do—muster her courage and show up at Smithson House unannounced. Whatever happened, she could handle it, as long as Rye took her back. They'd been together too long and had made too many future plans to let lies come between them.

The sun was setting as she drove the long live oak and oleander-lined driveway to the eight-sided house. She parked near the front door, praying she wasn't catching them during dinner. She only wanted to see Rye, no one else.

On the front porch, there was a blue plastic crate filled with garbage for recycling. When she raised her hand to knock, she noticed that the *Architectural Digest* book she'd given them lay on top of folded brown shopping bags and old catalogs. What cost her almost a full day's pay was being thrown out with the trash. Any shred of confidence, any feeling of worth she'd had just seconds before was replaced with the sure knowledge that she was no better than that stupid book. She'd been trying to be something she wasn't. She was trash.

There was no use knocking. She already had her answer.

The drive back to the marsh was filled with images of Junie drunk on the pier, Junie in the rocking chair spitting tobacco, and old photos of Junie when she was young and gorgeous. What if Krista ended up just like her? What if there was nothing she could do about it?

Chapter Eleven

JUNIE WAS IN the kitchen, her tin of bacon grease next to the stove. She was probably cooking eggs in the salty fat, seeing as there was a limited menu of what the woman was willing to spend time preparing. Krista was seven, maybe eight, and Zach was just a little guy who spent most of his time outside digging holes, fishing, or waging war with plastic army men. Krista was up early, wearing the pink bathing suit she wore every day during the summer in case she felt like jumping off the dock for a swim. No one came to visit them way out there on the marsh, not even other Hassells. Aunt Alice was next door, but she was really only in case of emergency. She liked to keep to herself, aside from an occasional wave when she was out in the back wearing her house dress and tending to her roses.

Krista's second-grade teacher, Mrs. Gamble, had come over for a wellness check. She was a big-nosed woman with short dark hair and a hard, trim figure. She wore colorful dresses and long necklaces that swung side to side as she walked around the room or wrote on the chalkboard. Krista knew who she was the minute she saw her sitting at their kitchen table.

She'd been vying for the woman's attention since the beginning of the year—hoping to be the lucky student who got to hold her hand on the way to the playground or the one she called on in class who, if they got the answer right, would be tossed a Jolly Rancher. Maybe Mrs. Gamble brought a candy with her, knowing how much Krista liked them and how rarely she actually got one. Krista ran for her, thrusting herself into the woman's lap, happier than a kitten on a teat that her teacher had come to visit.

"Excuse me, young lady," Mrs. Gamble said, placing Krista back onto the floor and brushing invisible dirt off her skirt. "I did not give you permission to touch me."

"Did you bring me a candy?" Krista jumped up and down, her hands together in hopeful prayer.

"Now why would I do that?" There was no smile on her face like there sometimes was for the other students. "Do you deserve a candy?"

Krista's excitement faded away. It was becoming clear that Mrs. Gamble was not happy to be there.

"Go outside," Daddy bellowed at her.

"But my teacher's here."

"Now," he said, pointing toward the back door.

If she didn't do as she was told, she'd be picking a switch and her backside would soon be on fire. She sulked her way outside, only instead of joining Zachy by the water's edge, she hid herself on the back stairs. They couldn't see her from the window, but she could hear much of what they said.

"Your child shows up filthy to school each day," Mrs. Gamble said. "It is not hygienic. Are you even able to care for her? It is my duty to contact Child Protective Services if I find you are neglecting your parental duties."

"What do you mean by that? You're gonna try to take my kids away?" Junie spoke to Mrs. Gamble with the mean voice she usually saved for her husband.

Several terse words later, a shadow filled the kitchen window, and a quick peek showed that her teacher was watching Zachy play outside. "What is wrong with your son?"

His legs didn't work well anymore. He had to lift them from his hips, which made him wobbly and off-kilter.

"Nothing is wrong with my son," Daddy said.

The teacher's voice got so low and serious that Krista couldn't make out what she was saying. Finally, she heard footsteps heading toward the front door.

"I suggest you take better care of your children, Mr. and Mrs. Hassell. I see that you are feeding them, and they do have a roof over their heads, but you are perilously close to losing them to the state."

"You stay away from my family, ya hear?" Daddy yelled. "I will pop a cap in your ass if you mess with us."

The footsteps stopped. "I will certainly report your threat, Mr. Hassell. Make sure your children are bathed before they return to school. And comb your daughter's hair."

She didn't even say goodbye. Krista tried to run her fingers through her matted hair and they got stuck halfway through. She noticed the black underneath her fingernails and the dirt between her toes. Mrs. Gamble was right. No one else at school was dirty like her. Her family was not like everyone else. But that's what happened at the marsh. There was so much to do and see outside that a person just plain got dirty. And the shower was cold and the water was rusty brown, so Mama just let her get on with things instead of putting up with her fussing about taking a bath.

Daddy stormed through the house, and before she could run off, he found Krista sitting on the back steps. Grabbing her by the back of her bathing suit, he carried her like a carpetbag to the bathroom, where he dumped her in the iron bathtub and turned on the freezing cold water. "If that devil woman ever comes to my house again, you'll get so many licks that you'll never sit again." He threw a bar of soap into her lap and left.

Krista heard him screaming at Junie, and Junie screaming back. Then the front door opened, the blue car started, and nobody saw Daddy again for a week.

From that day forward, Krista scrubbed herself clean every night. Sometimes she took the soap to the marsh because the water was warmer. She scrubbed Zachy, too. That night, Mama spent hours combing the knots out of her daughter's hair. Krista had no tears left by the time Mama was done tugging and pulling. But from then on, every morning Junie put Krista's long, fine hair in one long braid that hung down her back. None of it had mattered before Mrs. Gamble came over. Now, nothing would ever be the same again.

Chapter Twelve

IT'D BEEN ALMOST a week, and Krista hadn't heard a word from Rye. She was lonelier than ever, and the days at Tea and Tennyson dragged on. At least she had her online classes to fill some of the time. After the shop closed, she sat in the empty building to use the Wi-Fi and finish her homework. Her community college career was slow since she could pay for only one or two classes at a time, but she'd at least get an associate degree…eventually. She'd be the first in her family to do it, too.

It was early evening, she'd been studying since she locked the door at four, and her growling stomach reminded her that it was time for dinner. There was a restaurant downtown that had the most delicious pastrami pretzel sandwiches topped with white cheese and a beer-mustard glaze. Birdie brought one in for her once, and ever since then, she'd been craving another. Did she dare spend the money? She shook the study-daze from her head and stretched her legs. Maybe if she ate only half, then saved the rest for another meal, she could justify the cost.

Locking the door behind her, she crossed the street to the

courthouse. Behind the big red brick building was Crickley's small restaurant row. The upscale diner that sold her sandwich was smack in the middle.

Despite the heat, summer was her favorite time of year. She relished the sun still high at six P.M. and the sweet humidity that hung in the air all night long. Her long, tanned legs moved slowly, taking short strides and lacking a sense of urgency. It was a weeknight. There shouldn't be crowds at the restaurants. She could take her time and enjoy the colorful hibiscus that popped up every year just as the camellias dropped off, and the ruby-throated hummingbirds that loved them.

Scruggs had country music playing that day at work, and the last song was still stuck in her head. She hummed to the tune of "Fancy Like" as she passed a red-and-white barber's pole, and all of the patrons in black smocks watched her walk by from behind the glass. She allowed herself a small smile because she could see her reflection and she looked as good as any model in a magazine.

When she finally arrived at the diner, she was practically salivating at the thought of the sandwich to come. She opened the door and stepped across the threshold, pulling her wallet from her small purse. The hostess stand was in front of her, and at the table behind it sat Rye. With Miranda Nix. Her wallet fell to the floor. She grabbed it and ran out the door before the hostess asked for her name.

In a flash, she was back in high school. It had been one

of her best Fridays ever. She had her driver's license, her dad's old Mustang, and a good weekend weather forecast to fish and lay in the sun. Then Miranda Nix, out of the blue, invited her to a party. Nobody ever invited her to parties. Halloween was coming up, and Miranda emphasized that it was a costume party. Of course, Krista didn't have a costume unless she could go as a fisherman or an orphan. And there was no way she would show up as either.

It was as if Miranda could read her mind. "Wanna borrow a costume?" she asked.

"What is it?" Secretly, Krista hoped she would say Cinderella.

"A disco dancer. It's totally cool. I have the outfit in my locker from the dance show. Just add some crazy makeup and it'll be perfect." She opened her locker and handed Krista a bag.

"Thanks." She could hardly believe her luck. Most of the time, she was completely ignored, and now she was going to a party. She opened the bag and found a short silver-sequined dress. It really was cool, like Miranda said. She could hardly wait to put it on.

Zipping home with the windows down, she felt like her time had finally come. She'd hoped and prayed high school would be different, and now, not only had she just started dating Rye Smithson, she was about to make friends, too. It took only one girl to accept her, then the rest would follow. She'd seen it before. Thank God for Miranda Nix.

After borrowing Junie's eye shadow and following a YouTube video for colorful 1970s makeup, Krista thought she looked great. Surely, the girls would be impressed.

As she walked up to Miranda's front door that evening, she was more on edge than a tight-rope walker. The house was quiet, but she assumed that meant everyone was in the backyard. A few cars were parked in the driveway. She rang the doorbell, and Miranda answered with three of Krista's classmates standing behind her.

"Hi!" Krista said.

"What are you doing here?" Miranda asked.

"I'm here for the party. It's tonight, right?" She'd gone over the details a million times in her mind and was positive she had the correct day, time, and place.

"What party? There is no party," Miranda said. She was a very bad actor. "And if there was, you wouldn't be invited."

Krista's heart fell like a duck shot from the sky.

The girls behind Miranda giggled as they held up their phones to record her humiliation. All she could do was stand still, in shock.

"What are you supposed to be?" Miranda asked. "A stripper?"

"This is your dress," Krista said. "You let me borrow it."

"Bless your heart," Miranda said. "You have gone and lost your mind. I've never seen that thing before in my life."

She couldn't let them see her cry. "You are horrible," she squeaked before running back to her car.

Krista heard more laughter before the front door slammed.

Just remembering the event made her heart hurt for the girl she used to be—the stomach aches before school and all of the times she pretended not to hear what people were saying about her. Even the grown-ups—parents and teachers—treated her like she was destined to be either in jail or on the streets. The injustice of it made her so angry she wanted to scream.

She'd burned Miranda's silver dress in a fire by the marsh that night. Now she wanted to throw flames onto both of them, burn them to a crisp where they sat. She continued walking back toward the store.

"Krista!" It was Rye's voice. "Krista! Stop!"

She slowed long enough to look back. He was alone, so she stopped, allowing him to catch up. There was no use trying to cover up the hurt on her face. She let it show, hoping he would care.

"It's not what it looks like," he said. "We're not on a date."

"Why would it matter? You broke up with me."

"Yeah. And I'm still pissed as hell at you."

She didn't know what to say. Why Miranda Nix, of all people? "You've got it all wrong, Rye. You're punishing both of us because you won't hear the truth."

Up went his hand for the countdown again. "No card? No sparklers? No lies?" He held up a fourth finger. "No douchebag in North Charleston?"

"No. And I only lied because I was afraid you wouldn't understand—and I was right."

Miranda stepped outside of the restaurant. She was tall and thin with long, dark hair, but something had always been off with her looks. She was almost pretty, but not quite. "Rye!" she yelled, her hands on her hips.

"Just a second!" he shouted back.

"I will not wait for you!" Miranda threatened.

Rye seemed torn. "We're broken up," he said as much for himself as for Krista. "So you can't be mad at me."

"You never hear a word I say," Krista replied. "Enjoy your date."

"It's not a date." Then, as if disproving his words on the spot, he sprinted across the road and ushered Miranda back inside the restaurant.

Krista walked back to her car. She no longer wanted the sandwich, and she was done with Rye Smithson and Miranda Nix and every other judgmental, lying, selfish person on all of planet Earth. She had to stop getting into situations that made her feel like a loser. Something had to change.

Chapter Thirteen

"YOU'RE A MESS," Birdie said.

Krista had been stung by a bee while cleaning the outside tables and was holding a penny to the spot on her arm that was quickly beginning to swell.

"That old wives' tale won't work," Birdie pointed out. "You need you some meat tenderizer."

"I'll be okay."

"Let us at least put some spit on it." Birdie put out her hand, coughed, and spat.

"No! Birdie! Gross." She pulled her pennied arm away from Birdie's loogie.

"Don't be ridiculous. My saliva is like magic."

"No, thank you."

Birdie brought her wet hand up near Krista's arm again.

"No, thank you. No, thank you!" Krista yelled as she jerked away.

"For heaven's sake," Birdie said, wiping the spit on a napkin. "I'm just helping you."

"That's the kind of help that leads to amputation," Scruggs said, bringing Birdie her afternoon cookie.

"Hush it, Scribble-face." She took her cookie and waved him away. "Now, Krista. I have been hearing things."

Of course she had. The woman had ears like a bat and a vampire's thirst for gossip. "I'm told that your boy Rye was out with Miranda Nix last night."

"I am aware."

"Are you also aware that she has made it clear she has designs on him?"

"This does not surprise me, Birdie." She knew it in her heart, but it hurt to hear out loud. "What am I supposed to do about it?"

"That is an excellent question. See, I used to think it was in your best interest to fight for him. He's got a stable family, a strong future. But I don't know. I'm startin' to buck that idea. Not sure why. Maybe it's because that ol' Johnny Merrick is a flavor."

"Johnny Merrick is a drunken dipshit who thinks he's better than everybody else." Krista rolled her eyes. "I can't believe you'd even bring him up. He's from *Chicago*."

"Oooooh," Birdie whistled. "She's cussing now. That there means something."

"It means I strongly dislike him."

"Right. Sure it does."

Between the pain in her arm and Birdie's obtuse lack of tact, Krista was weakening. Seeing Rye with Miranda had been downright excruciating. The old feelings of hopelessness, frustration, humiliation, and sadness blended together as anger and mixed with the poison from the bee sting. But there was no place for any of it to go. Krista's whole body shook.

"Oh, honey," Birdie said, reaching for her. "Are you having an allergic reaction?"

"Don't hug me," she said. "I'm fine. I need you to go away."

Birdie wouldn't hear of it. She forcibly hugged her, holding tight to Krista's stiff form until she finally bent.

"I don't want your pity, Birdie." Krista could barely speak.

"Only the pitiful need pity, and that is not you," Birdie said, squeezing Krista harder into her fleshy body.

It took more than a minute of forceful hugging before the compassion, the humanity, broke her down, and Krista sobbed into Birdie's shoulder, her words short and staccato with breaths in between. "I don't know what to do."

"I'll tell you what you do," Birdie said. "Stop fighting the old, and start building the new. You don't need Rye Smithson anymore."

Scruggs, who was always listening, jumped in. "I don't know why you stayed with that loser anyway. You should've dumped him when you moved to Myrtle Beach."

Krista gently let go of Birdie and agreed with Scruggs, wiping her face with a handful of napkins. "He just felt…important is all," she said. "He still does."

"Sounds like that's more about you and less about him,"

Scruggs said. He pulled his shoulders back like he had just made the statement of the century.

Birdie interrupted. "Who are you, Buddha?"

Scruggs ignored her. "I will tell you right now, Rye Smithson is not important. The way I see it, you can either shut down or grow up. Which one is it gonna be?"

Krista was no longer shaking. He was reinforcing what she already knew. Something had to change. There was no option to shut down. Her brother needed her. Her mother needed her.

She was going to have to grow up. And she was going to have to do it without Rye.

"YOU'RE MY BEST friend," Krista said, holding Zach's limp hand on the front porch of the beach house. They'd brought another small rosebush from home and planted it before going inside. There was no need for conversation anymore. Just being together was enough.

A breeze blew sand over the tops of the dunes, and the insects sounded like buzzing electrical wires.

Zach tried speaking. "I like Johnny."

"You did not just say that."

A slight smile lit his face.

"Why is everybody saying that to me today? There is nothing to like about that guy."

"Better than Rye."

"You think so?" She dropped his hand and moved over to the porch swing, leaving him alone in his wheelchair. The sound of tires blended with the ocean before they both realized that someone was coming. Zach strained his eyes to the left, unable to move his head. Krista walked to the end of the porch, shielding her eyes from the setting sun.

"Who is it?" Zach asked.

"Can't tell."

Even though it was a private island, it was not patrolled by law enforcement. Anyone could ignore the signs and trespass. The brother and sister who owned the island, Jack and Charlotte, had been talking about installing a gate at the entrance of the bridge, but they hadn't done it yet.

"I think the car is white," she said, squinting. "Should I get you inside?"

"Why?"

"I don't know. Just in case."

"No."

She held her breath. Who did she know with a white car? Not Birdie, not Rye, not Scruggs. It looked like a new Mercedes. What kind of murderer drove a Mercedes? Certainly, they wouldn't want to get blood in the car.

She couldn't see through the tinted windows until the car pulled up right next to the house. A handsome man dressed head to toe in a designer suit stepped out. Jackson Buchanan.

"Hey, y'all!" he said.

"Hey, Jack!" Krista hoped that he knew his sister Charlotte had given her permission to use the beach house. Charlotte owned the half of the island they were on, but Jack owned the other half.

"Y'all good?" he asked, coming up onto the porch and patting Zach on the shoulder.

"Just enjoying the nice evening," she said.

"Oh, I know. I hate to bother you. I've got to close up the house for the storm."

"Is there one coming?"

"She's churning down near the Gulf now. Could be a hurricane. Can't be too careful."

Krista looked south, as if she'd be able to see the weather from so far away. "I'll help," she said.

Together they flipped in the storm shutters and locked them closed, then put all the planters and outdoor furniture in the garage and locked the doors. When the house was as protected as possible, Jack helped Krista get Zach into the car.

"Thanks for the help getting the house ready," he said before closing Zach's door. "You're good people."

"You're welcome," she said. Good people? That seemed like a strange thing to say. But he was right. Being poor didn't make a person bad, just like money didn't make a person good. Money just made things easier. Krista felt her gumption grow. She was a good person. No matter what other people said.

Chapter Fourteen

IT WAS OVERCAST that day; the front end of the category one hurricane that hit Florida the day before was slowly moving north. It churned over the Atlantic, building up power. Rain was spittin' on and off that night, so Krista stationed buckets under the leaky spots inside her house. Surely, Rye was planning to ride out the storm in his two-thousand-square-foot hunting cabin. He'd be drinking whiskey with his buddies and watching the weather roll in. She closed the ancient half-broken wooden shutters on the backside of the house facing the marsh. If the winds ramped up, their single-pane windows might not survive it. Junie was on the old couch on the back porch drinking a beer, with Zach in his wheelchair watching raindrops hit the marsh. She'd promised Krista that she would not go out to the bars, even though the full force of the storm wasn't supposed to hit for another day.

Krista considered telling them about Rye. They were bound to hear about it soon, anyway. Yet somehow, despite Miranda Nix, their breakup didn't feel final. Maybe because everything it was based upon was false. Maybe because he'd chased after her when she saw him at the restaurant. Surely, he would figure out how unfair he'd been and apologize. It would be a great day when that happened. To have Rye groveling to her, wanting her back, admitting that he'd made a mistake—the thought of it almost made her giddy. He'd gone against his family and pulled her out of the trash heap once before. He could do it again. And this time, Miranda would be the one left alone. She hummed while she pulled the lawn chairs up to the shed, her hair blowing in all directions and sticking to the sweat on her brow.

"You need some help?"

She turned with a smile that quickly died. It was Johnny, standing there looking tanned and cocky.

"No," she said.

He walked down and grabbed a faded lawn chair, its plastic webbing coming apart, and followed her to the shed.

"I said no," she said. "I don't want any help."

"I'm back from Chicago." He grabbed the chair from her hands and easily stacked them both in the old wooden building.

"I can see that."

"Your house is pretty low to the ground," he pointed out.

She ignored him.

"Are you planning to sit out the storm?"

"We're planning to monitor it," she answered. She wanted to know his plans but wasn't going to pretend to care by asking.

"It might get bad. There might be flooding," he said.

"I know what the weather is like out here," she said. "And if you're so worried, maybe you should've stayed in Chicago." She picked up an old bucket and tossed it onto the pile of chairs.

He chuckled at her orneriness, standing in the middle of her path back to the house. "The boondocks are kinda growing on me."

"Maybe you ought to get a prescription for that." She walked around him and stomped back toward the house. He stuck with her. "Why are you following me?"

"I need to talk to your mother."

"There is nothing you can say to her that you can't say to me."

"You won't listen to me."

Krista turned and stood smack in front of him. She felt like a scrappy Chihuahua in a face off with a Great Dane. "I'm listening."

He grinned down at her, then called out over the top of her head, "Mrs. Hassell?"

Junie's voice answered. "Yes? Who is that?"

"It's your neighbor, Johnny."

"Well, welcome back, honey. Come on up here and let me see your face."

Johnny stepped around Krista.

Junie's eyes lit up the minute she laid them on him.

"Well, hello, handsome."

"Mrs. Hassell." He extended his hand to shake hers. His head was awfully close to the ceiling of the screened-in porch.

Junie didn't move from the old sofa, just leaned her chest over so that her breasts rested on her knees as she daintily took his hand. Her white T-shirt was so thin that her lacy black bra was visible underneath. "Is business good back in Chicago?"

"Yes, ma'am," he said.

Krista was sure that he purposefully used the word *ma'am* just to annoy her. They didn't say that in Illinois.

"Pardon me," Junie said, "but I see you're wearing an army T-shirt. Are you military?"

"Yes, ma'am. Well, I used to be."

Krista rolled her eyes. Zach was straining with interest, clearly pleased by the visit, so she tried to dial down her annoyance.

Zach tried to speak. "What…branch?" He'd always loved the military—all of his favorite movies involved war scenes.

"Army. I fought with Will Rushton and Jack Buchanan in Afghanistan."

"Oh my." Junie feigned with a hand on her heart, giving him the works. "You are a bona fide hero."

Please don't say thank you for your service, Krista prayed.

"Thank you for your service," Junie said.

Krista went inside where she could still hear the conversation but didn't have to be a part of the agony of it. She let the door slam behind her.

"It's my pleasure, ma'am," he said, ignoring the interruption. "Listen, if this storm gets any worse, you are all welcome to come next door. That house is made of tabby, and from what I understand, that old mixture of oyster shells, lime, and sand is effective at keeping out the sea. Plus, it's built up ten feet."

Did he not realize that he was describing the house to the people who'd lived next door to it their entire lives? Of course they knew it was raised and made of tabby. He was an idiot.

"I just loaded up on food and bottled water," he went on, clearly feeling extra charitable that day. "You can just keep the key and come in whenever you need to."

"Well, if you ain't just the best kind of gentleman. Thank you, darlin'." Junie was all smiles. "We might have to take you up on your offer."

Over my dead body.

With her ear to the door, she heard Johnny start to leave. "Bye, Zach, nice seeing you again."

Why couldn't that man just leave them alone? She wanted things to be normal. She wanted her old peaceful life back without some guy coming over to scare them and make them feel like they weren't living right. Like they weren't good enough.

KRISTA DROVE TO work in a dark, early morning downpour. It was nothing special; she'd been through plenty of thunderstorms. The weather wasn't oppressive and heavy like a tornado might be brewing. As a matter of fact, if she didn't know better, she would swear the storm would blow over by the afternoon.

Parking closer to the store than she normally would, she was grateful for the light of the early morning streetlamps. Not many people would be coming to the shop in this weather, so she didn't feel bad about using up a prime parking space. It was too windy for her umbrella, so she pulled the hood of her black raincoat over her head and made a run for the front door.

There was no way to avoid puddles, but she was able to unlock the door and get into the store with her hair still dry, so that was a win. By the time she had all of the lights turned on, Scruggs and Emma showed up holding hands as they ran through the rain together, with Waffles's head peeking out from underneath Scruggs's jacket. Despite all that was going on, seeing those two falling in love warmed her heart. That anyone could see through Scruggs's sarcasm to the kindhearted guy underneath was nothing short of a miracle.

Krista checked her phone to see if her mother had returned any of her texts. Contrary to her promise, Junie had snuck out again last night. There was no sign of her that morning, so Krista was forced to leave Zach home alone. He was sound asleep when she left, but Junie had better get home soon. He needed to be cleaned and fed and put into his wheelchair.

Worrying about Zach took up too much space in Krista's brain. The forgetfulness was especially noticeable when her job was to put various specific ingredients into cups for discriminating people. After she made a full-caf vanilla latte for a no-caf mocha customer, she finally asked Scruggs to make the drinks while she took over the register. Emma was on bookstore and table-cleaning duty, which, in retrospect, Krista should've been doing instead. She was supposed to be a smiling face to greet the customers, but was so sick with worry over Zach that she could do nothing but scowl. One man even asked her if her dog had just died.

She'd been there for four hours with four more to go when she finally burst. "I have to go," she said to Scruggs and Emma. "Zachy's all alone and Mama won't text me back." The wind kicked up and pushed open the front door as if Mother Nature was agreeing that she needed to go home immediately.

"Go," Scruggs said.

"We've got this," said Emma.

Krista ran out, nearly slipping on the wet pavement, not bothering to shield her hair from the rain on the way to her car. The deluge had picked up strength, and the street drainage was backing up into deep puddles reaching the crest of the curb.

"I'm coming, Zachy," she said under her breath as she eased her old car from its flooded parking spot. Her only worry was of Zach being awake, hungry, and soiled, with no one around to help. Without the use of his hands, he couldn't call anyone. The house would be loud with water seeping through the roof into the buckets, the casings on their old windows squeaking and whistling like they did with every storm. She wasn't worried about flooding. The marsh protected them from floods. It absorbed water like a sponge, letting it spill out slowly. She was just worried about Zachy.

Hang in there, little buddy.

It took twice as long as usual, her windshield wipers barely able to keep up with the steady onslaught. She heard nothing but the endless pounding rain and splashing until her tires finally ran over the weedy gravel beside her house. In a flash, she was inside, leaving a trail of water as she ran straight to Zach's room. The electricity had gone out, and his room was dark, the bed empty.

"Zachy?" She hadn't seen her mother's old truck out front. "Mama?"

There was no answer. She ran to the back porch in case they were huddled behind the screens watching the weather. A piece of paper on the round oak table in the kitchen caught her eye. It was a note.

KRISTA,

ZACH IS NEXT DOOR WITH ME. HE'S SAFE. COME

OVER.

JOHNNY

Fury rose hot and swift in her chest. How dare he trespass. How dare he violate her privacy. Zach was *her* responsibility. *Her* brother. Johnny Merrick needed to keep his nose the hell out of other people's business. She felt like he'd just caught her committing a crime. It was like he was trying to catch her at her worst.

Krista ran down the back stairs, leaving the screen door to slam shut behind her. The edge of the marsh had swollen past where the lawn chairs used to be. In her entire life, she'd never seen the water rise that high before. She looked into the blackened sky for the sun, as if finding it would tell her if the king tide was on its way. But she already knew it was coming. People had been talking about it for a while. The full moon and the alignment of it, the earth, and the sun, was expected to result in an exceptionally high tide. That, and storm surge together could be devastating. Slipping her way through the muddy, patchy weeds and trees between the houses, she finally made it to the old tabby retaining wall protecting Aunt Alice's backyard garden, the pink of her Savannah roses somehow more vibrant in the wetness. "Zach!" she yelled. The back door opened as she entered the garden. Johnny stood tall at the entrance.

"Get in here," he said, putting his hand on her back as she reached the top and ushering her in. It was bright yellow inside, lights on in every room, with Zach stationed in his wheelchair, dry and happy, in front of a television playing *Family Feud.*

Krista went straight to her brother and hugged his head. "You okay?"

"Good," he said, the tiniest hint of a smile on his face.

"I'm so sorry. I never should have left you."

"It's okay."

"Danged Mama. I don't even know where she is."

"Shhhhh," he said in his slow, whispered voice. "It's fi-ne."

She didn't want to look in Johnny's direction. Didn't want to thank him for her brother being dry and, from the smell of things, clean. The minute she walked into the house, her anger disappeared. But she still didn't want to be grateful. She couldn't allow herself to be vulnerable around him.

"Did he feed you?" she asked as if Johnny wasn't standing right there.

"Yes, I brought over all of his cans," Johnny said. "I've got food for us, too, plenty of water, and the generator's up and running."

Krista finally looked at him. "You broke into my house." As she said it, she felt like a jerk.

He looked taken aback. "I walked in through the back door."

"Kiki," Zach said. "Stop."

"Well, now you need to move him back home." If she

showed him any weakness, she would break. She had to be mad at him. She had to.

Johnny laughed. He *laughed*. "Within twenty-four hours, your house will be flooded. I will go back with you and help you get anything you want. But I will not take your brother back there."

"Listen, our house has been standing for more than fifty years. It has never flooded. The marsh does not flood."

"Krista. Things aren't like they used to be. The sea level has risen throughout the entire Lowcountry. All it will take is one tidal surge."

Her voice was getting shaky the deeper she dug herself in. "Is this what I get for helping you? You're holding my little brother hostage?" She stood defensively. She knew she was picking a fight. The man had helped her, and she was purposefully twisting up his good deed and hitting him with it.

Zach began moaning. "Stop," he said again.

Johnny stepped back. He pulled out a kitchen chair and sat down. "I hear you," he said. "When you put it that way, it does look like I'm keeping him here against your will."

Krista was immediately disarmed. He wasn't supposed to agree with her. He was supposed to call her names, to remind her of her position in society. She wanted him to say it all out loud, to scream it at her so that she could fight back.

"Zach and I've been talking," he said. "I told him the

whole story. Right, Zach?"

"Yes," Zach drew out.

"See, I can't sleep. I haven't gotten a good night's sleep in four years. I heard your mother leave last night. I heard you leave this morning. I got worried. I was trying to help."

The wind blew a loud spray of water onto the entire back of the house like a full blast garden hose, and they all jumped.

"The marsh is not going to flood," she said. It was one last weak attempt to get at him.

"Let's go move your car to higher ground," Johnny said.

She made no move to leave.

"Just in case, okay?"

Zach stared at her. Despite his lack of expression, she knew the look in eyes very well. He was pleading with her to listen. She shouldn't have put Zach through all of the drama.

She nodded toward Johnny, who was already at the coat closet pulling out a large army-green raincoat.

"Put this on," he said, holding out the jacket like he was a gentleman helping a lady with her mink coat. Krista walked over and put her arms in the too-long sleeves.

Without saying a word, the two braved the weather to save her car and whatever else they could from her house.

Just in case.

Chapter Fifteen

JOHNNY WAS WRONG, of course. The marsh would never flood. Sea level or not, some things in the South would never change. Krista kept trying to convince herself of it, but her instincts battled with her brain while her whole body tingled on high alert.

She sat at his dinner table with no makeup left on her face and her hair drying into a frizzy lion's mane. No one seemed to notice. There was nothing she could do about it, anyway.

She didn't mean for it to happen, but as the night wore on and the storm raged outside, it began to feel like Johnny, Zach, and she were the only people in the world. They were safe, huddled together in the clean, bright kitchen, with two suitcases full of clothes, Krista's laptop, some documents, a wooden chess game made by her grandfather, the family Bible, and all of their photo albums. She wore the only jewelry she had of any value—a necklace from her grandmother and a bracelet Rye had given her for Christmas one year. Her mother was surely wearing her only piece of jewelry, her wedding ring, wherever she might be. None of the men Junie hooked up with cared that she wore one.

Thankfully, Johnny wasn't drinking. There was no tequila to be seen. The only tantrum being thrown was by the storm outside.

She won at poker and laughed at his stories about pranking Will Rushton in college. Her belly was full of crackers and vegetable beef stew. And most of all, Zach was happy and relaxed, like he finally had the friend he'd been praying for. In the hours before bed, Krista unwittingly softened more. Not in a chatty sort of way, but in the quiet way that happened when you'd decided someone was not evil, and that you probably owed them an apology. He'd passed every test she'd thrown at him, and had never made himself bigger or unsheathed his claws when she poked at him. He deserved some credit for that.

Johnny helped get Zach ready for bed. They tucked him snuggly into Aunt Alice's four-poster bed in the downstairs room off the family room, and covered him with a lavender-smelling sheet and a soft patchwork quilt. There was no sound of a leaking roof and no whistling windows, just rain and wind against what felt like a fortress. She said good night to Johnny and climbed in beside her brother. Listening to Zach's shallow breathing and the timed puffs of air from the oxygen machine, Krista stared up at the sharp white corners of the ceiling.

There was an old wives' tale that if you named the four corners of a room, whichever one you woke up facing was the name of the man you would marry. She'd given names to corners before, only the last time, she'd cheated. She'd named all four corners Rye, as if the old wives could somehow be tricked and the tale would still hold true. This time she did it right. She named the far corner for Rye, chose two random names—Jason and Nathan—for the corners behind her, and named the fourth corner, the one to the right of the door, after Johnny. She flushed when she looked at Johnny's corner, both embarrassed and strangely hopeful that she would wake up facing it.

There was no telling how long she slept. It had turned darker than outer space in their room, and for a moment Krista was disoriented. A siren whooped and screeched in the distance. Zach gasped with fear beside her. The door opened, and before she could sit up, Johnny had his arms underneath Zach's body, lifting him from the bed while barking orders at her. "Get upstairs!"

Still dressed in the sweatpants and T-shirt she'd changed into after getting soaked, she jumped up and did as she was told. Her ears popped and a mouse ran across the floor right by her bare feet at the bottom of the stairs. Johnny was ahead of her, carrying Zach and moving swiftly. "Do you have your phone?" he asked.

She'd thought to grab it off the nightstand on her way out. "Yes."

"Set off the emergency signal."

She double-clicked the side buttons and swiped to send

an SOS.

"Don't worry! This house can withstand a ten-foot storm surge. Maybe more." He was yelling over the loud, strange sounds of wood cracking and waves crashing against the house.

"The marsh doesn't flood!" Krista yelled.

The entire top floor was the master bedroom. Johnny deposited Zach on the king-sized bed, organizing the pillows to make him comfortable. He ran to the window where Krista was already peering outside. The cracking wood was coming from the direction of her house. Outside, beneath Aunt Alice's old garden retaining wall, wooden planks bearing flaking white paint, and one of Junie's kitchen chairs, were being carried out to a marsh that was no longer thick with spartina grass but had instead turned into a whitewater river.

"This can't be happening." She was too shocked to cry.

Johnny forcefully put his arm around her, pressing her cheek into the side of his chest. "It's going to be okay." Two cockroaches climbed the wall beside the window like they were trying to escape the surge, too.

"No, it's not," she said, pushing him away. "Even if we survive, that house is all we have." She left the warmth of Johnny and climbed into the large bed beside Zach's paralyzed body. He was completely immobile, his eyes as wide as the heartless full moon watching the destruction from up high. She snuggled into his body and put her arm around his waist, listening to the horrifying sounds of a home being battered and wondering if the old place would hold. Maybe it'd be better if the flood took them with it. Zach wasn't going to last much longer anyway. Her mother would have no place to live. And Krista? Maybe the fight was over. Rye was gone. They might as well be swept away. With Johnny manning the window, she stared straight ahead, her eyes glued to the right-hand corner of the room. It was then that she remembered. When the sirens went off, she had awakened facing the corner named Johnny.

He stood sentry, giving them a calm blow-by-blow of what was happening outside. Although the water was wicked and fast-moving, carrying all kinds of dangerous debris, it didn't appear to be rising any more. It hadn't touched Aunt Alice's roses. Krista pulled her phone from her pocket and texted her mother for the gazillionth time.

"WHERE ARE YOU?"

It was nearly three A.M., and this time Junie texted back. *"I'm fine. Leave me be."*

"Our house is gone. The flood took it." It may have been ruthless to be so blunt, but Junie deserved the shock.

Immediately, Krista's phone rang. "What are you talking about, our house is gone? Are you messing with me?"

"No, Mama. It's gone. Zachy and I are next door at Aunt Alice's."

"Shit."

Krista heard shuffling and things getting knocked over.

"Where are you?" she asked.

"Never you mind where I am. You go get that house back."

Krista held the phone from her ear and looked at it like it'd done lost its mind. "Good one, Mama. Very funny."

Then the wailing began. "What am I gonna do? That house is all I have. Good Lord, why are you punishing me? What have I done to deserve this?"

"We've got family, Mama. Surely, we can stay with somebody."

"I don't want to stay with those bastards. I hate them."

"That's not true and you know it."

"It is true. And don't you start lecturing me, now. You can just run off to Myrtle Beach whenever you want. Get yourself a little job and strut yourself around like you ain't got a care in the world. But I am *stuck*. Do you hear me? And now I am stuck here without a damn *house*." There was more shuffling around and a man's voice before Junie abruptly hung up.

"That went well," Krista said with dripping sarcasm. She turned to Zach. "You could hear what she said, couldn't you?"

"Mm-hmm," Zach said sadly, his breathing loud and labored despite the oxygen strapped to his nose.

She looked up at the darkened figure by the window, pretending not to be listening.

"We're not stuck, you know." She kissed Zach on the

side of his head. "We love you so much."

He attempted the smallest smile, but she couldn't help notice the dampness on his face and pillow. She found a tissue box on the bedside table and wiped his cheeks and nose. "You are everything to me. Don't you worry, okay?"

Johnny still said nothing, just continued watching the water outside.

"I will put a roof over our heads if it means building it myself." They were big words for a young woman who had neither the money, skills, nor time to do such a thing. Zach would require a place to live immediately, and there was no way she could provide it for him.

Whatever had been normal before that moment would never be again. There would be no more familiar bed, no more too-hot oven or off-kilter fan, no more screened-in porch when the June bugs stuck to everything, no more buckets in a rainstorm, or Mama sitting on the old couch in her bed clothes dipping chaw and complaining. No more marsh for any of them.

Krista was going to have to swallow her pride and ask for help. And she would have to do it as soon as the flood receded.

Chapter Sixteen

KRISTA HAD TRUSTED the marsh. She'd loved the marsh. And it had betrayed her so violently, she wanted to lash out at it. For twenty-four years she had lived on its banks in harmony with the ebb and flow of its tides. She'd counted on it to protect her, to feed her, to…love her back.

She did her best to talk herself down, to accept the reality that was before her. It wasn't personal, she told herself. But it sure felt like it as she stared out at the roiling water carrying off bits and pieces of her life. If people really did reap what they sowed, she would have to start sowing more good things. Enough to make up for her family and for whatever she'd done to make the marsh so mad.

Working hard to set her disappointment aside, she tried to stay in the moment. Thinking too far ahead was painful. In addition to a dry, intact house, Krista and Zach were lucky to have Johnny's generator. Because of it, she was able to charge her phone. And because of that, she was able to answer when Rye called. She left Zach and Johnny in the master bedroom and walked downstairs to talk. The waters had receded, and even though it was still raining, she knew from the radar app that the worst of the storm had passed.

Finally, she could let her guard down and cry. Rye had been with her so long that he knew how few material items she had and how much that house meant to her. She needed their shared history in that moment, so she let her emotions flow. She told him how her house was gone, how the roar of the surge and the winds beating against the walls and windows had been so frightening. He listened, and said he was happy she was okay. As she'd guessed, he'd been at his lodge drinking whiskey. He even thought about going out in the rain to shoot him some wood ducks because he knew where they would be hiding from the storm.

"Listen," he said. "I have some good news for you. I got to thinking that maybe you're actually only at strike two."

Krista said nothing. She wasn't sure she wanted to hear what he was about to say.

"I mean, you going to the grocery store to get compliments is weird as hell, but I get that not everybody's as nice to you as I am. I mean, I saw with my own two eyes that you were all dressed up that day, and I saw that cupcake you brought for Zach. I believe I can see fit to trust you on that one."

"What are you saying?"

"I'm saying we can get back together. I will even try to say more nice things to you."

The stability and familiarity of his offer felt good. Her world was shifting back onto its axis—just enough to maintain some hope. After all, when she really needed him, he stepped up and called. She'd always known Rye was that guy.

"So, where are you?" he asked. "You at the store?"

"No, we're next door at Aunt Alice's." She prayed he wouldn't ask any more questions. Dread rose along with her blood pressure.

"Where the party was at on the Fourth?"

She desperately wanted to hold on to Rye. She needed him. But there was no way out of her predicament. All he had to do was check an app on his phone, and he could see exactly where she was. "I believe so," she said. Each word was like taking a step up to a noose.

"You believe so." He repeated her slowly, malice in his voice. "And who do you believe is in the house with you right now?"

"Well, Zach, of course."

"And..."

And the stool was about to be kicked out from beneath her feet. "And, a guy from Chicago who is out here visiting. He's friends with Will Rushton. They were in the army together. He knows Jackson Buchanan and—"

"You gonna give me his social security number, too?" Rye's voice grew louder. "He's the guy from the wedding, right? The one who gave you the card and the stupid sparklers."

Krista's heart dropped. "Rye, babe, please don't yell at

me. He's our neighbor, and we needed help." Her body felt like Jell-O as she slumped onto the unmade bed. "I was going to stay at the house. I wasn't going to leave." Her voice sounded shaky and panicked.

"And yet, you left," he interrupted. "Didn't you? You marched yourself right on over to that guy's house."

"Well, yes. But only because it was an emergency."

Rye's chuckle was pure whiskey-laced sarcasm. "Three strikes, Krista. Three strikes."

She was unsure of what to say. A figure darkened the doorway, and she looked up to see Johnny. He was furious. "Let me talk to him."

Krista vehemently shook her head. "Please, Rye. It's all a big misunderstanding."

Johnny walked closer. "I will not let him treat you this way."

"Shhhh..." she said, waving him away.

"Are you talking to him right now?" Rye's voice got louder and faster. "Is that asshole right there with you?"

Johnny stood before her now, his hand outstretched toward her phone.

"I have to go," she said. "I'll call you later."

"The hell you will!" Rye said. "You are dead to me."

He hung up before Krista could. She nearly threw her phone at Johnny's head. "Why did you do that?" she yelled. "You just made everything so much worse!" She pulled a pillow to her face, muffling her screams of frustration, then threw it to the floor. "I don't want your help! I want you to leave me alone."

After an hour of sheer panic, stuck staring out the window watching the wood of her home float on the water, she calmed into the knowledge that Rye would rescue her. He just needed some time to recover from the shock that her neighbor was Johnny. Just like he'd decided to give her a second chance with the grocery store incident, he would come to understand that she'd had no choice. If Johnny hadn't forced them next door, she and Zach would be out there floating on the marsh along with her mother's collection of Cool Whip containers. Surely, Rye would realize that and be grateful she was alive. He had to. He was her best hope for a future.

Despite her SOS signal and her hope for Rye, when the sun came up, and all day long, no one came to Johnny's house. She and Johnny walked where they could, looking for anything salvageable from where her house used to stand. Even if they found a spoon or an old hammer, it hardly seemed worth saving. Dead animals, mostly fish and birds, lay strewn among the debris, and the marsh she'd trusted so much seemed passive, uninterested in her pain. She wanted to go to bed, pull up YouTube on her phone, and lose herself in other people's lives. Johnny agreed. There wasn't much else they could do, and it was clear that they wouldn't be going anywhere for a while.

He had plenty of bottled water, but they couldn't flush

the toilets or take a shower with no running water. They used buckets of marsh water to flush, and Johnny showed Krista how they showered in the army. It was simple—you lifted your arm and applied more deodorant. She laughed and borrowed his Right Guard, noting that it smelled like him.

Krista made an early supper that night—turkey sandwiches with a special sauce made from mayonnaise, pickle relish, and ketchup. They put towels on the Adirondack chairs in his garden and sat for hours, the air feeling like a steam shower and smelling like pluff mud and rot. Zach was stationed on the red brick patio next to them in his wheelchair. He was the first one to spot a firefly.

"You saw the first one *again*?" Krista laughed. "You have special lightning bug-spotting powers."

Zachy chuckled, which made him cough and choke. Krista jumped up to help, but the moment quickly passed. Zach grunted out numbers each time he saw another. It was like the first firefly had called the rest of them out of hiding, and soon, he was at seven. They blinked and hovered in all of the dark spaces.

"You're the lucky one again," Krista said. "You're always the lucky one."

Johnny wiped the sweat from his brow with the corner of the towel he sat on. "I wish the showers were working," he said, breaking up the choir of insect sounds. "It's what I do when I need to wash away the bullshit of the world."

"If that worked, I'd be in the shower all the time."

"It works if you let it." They were quiet again, watching the light show increase as the darkness set in.

"Why'd you move to the marsh, Johnny?" Krista asked. "Why'd you come here when you could have stayed near the beach or downtown?"

"I guess I was trying to get as far away from people as I could."

"Are there any particular people you were trying to get away from?"

He shrugged. "Not really. I don't have a wife or a girlfriend, if that's what you're asking. Never been married. I just needed to get away from my life in Chicago. From the stress. It was causing me problems."

"What kind of problems?"

"The kind that can be solved with hard work, time, and saltwater."

She sensed that he didn't want to say more. "I'll tell you how my mother solved problems," she said. "Pick your switch. That's how."

"Ah," Johnny said. "A purveyor of corporal punishment."

"Yep, we got licks for just about everything. Right, Zachy?" He blinked his eyes at her as if to say *yes*. "But it was always Mama. Daddy threatened all the time, but actually never hit us. Bad as that man might be, he never once laid a hand on me or Zach. He never hit Mama, neither."

Johnny reached over to where her arm rested on the chair and covered her hand with his. She left it there.

"In the army, do they teach you how to make people listen?" she asked. "I mean, I do everything I can to be a good person, to do things right, and no one cares. No one hears me. They don't believe what I say."

Johnny squeezed her hand. "Are you talking about your boyfriend?"

She nodded.

"I'm gonna tell you something, but don't get mad, okay?"

She probably deserved that. Johnny had been the circle board for many of her recent darts.

"I think part of the problem is that you keep forgiving someone who isn't sorry."

She sat with that. Mulling it over.

Johnny broke the silence. "You ready for bed, Zach?"

Together, they prepared him for bed and got him comfortable in the room off the kitchen. She wasn't tired at all. Johnny was in the family room, so she took the recliner next to him on the couch.

"You're supposed to forgive people," she said.

"Yes," he said. "But you do it for *you*, not for them. And, every time you forgive that jerk, it gives him permission to keep treating you like that."

She wanted to get mad at him. She wanted to lash out, but she knew in her heart he was right. "I need a shower," she said, leaning into the chair.

"We all do."

They each sat silently, scrolling through their phones, figuring out which areas had been hit by the hurricane and which had been lucky enough to avoid it. Johnny got up to get a bottle of water and peeked into the room where Zach slept. Then he walked all the way in. A second later, he yelled, "Krista! Get in here!"

Krista ran into the room, stopping at the foot of the bed. Zach was an eerie shade of blue. Johnny assessed to see if he was still breathing.

"Zachy!" She jumped onto the bed next to him and placed her hand on his cheek. "Little brother, please."

Zach took a shallow breath. "There you go, bud," Johnny said. "Keep breathing." The oxygen hose on his nose was emitting puffs, but Zach barely took them in. Krista looked straight into Johnny's eyes and what she saw there made everything worse.

She kneeled next to the bed and grabbed hold of Zach's arm, tears blurring her view of his face. "I love you so much. Zachy, you are the best little brother." She kissed his face all over. "I'm not ready for this. Please don't go. I love you so much. I love you. I love you."

Johnny walked out of the room. She heard him cuss, then the back door slammed.

She sat with Zach as his breaths came less often than they should. The hospice folks said it would be like this. Fish-out-of-water breathing, his skin changing color. She wasn't ready. She would never be ready.

The back door squeaked open, and Johnny appeared again. He was calm. Almost too calm. "Zach, can you blink?" he asked. They both studied Zach's eyes. It was slight, but they definitely blinked. Johnny turned to Krista. "He knows you love him. I promise you that. But I've been with soldiers as they took their last breaths and here's what they all wanted, and what Zach wants now: for you to know that *he* loves *you*. Right, bud?" Again, a barely perceptible blink. "Think about it. Think about what you would want if you were him."

"Zachy," she whispered, stroking the cheek on his open-mouthed face, so familiar, so adored. "Blink twice if you love me."

It was as clear as day. He squeezed his eyelids tightly together two times.

"I see you," she said, brushing the hair from his forehead. "You love me. I'll tell Mama you love her, too."

He blinked twice again.

"It's okay, bud," Johnny said, his voice strong. "It's okay to go. I will make sure your mother and your sister are okay. I promise."

With an abnormally long exhale, no more breaths came. Just like that. They waited and waited for an inhale, like Zach was a resurrection fern that, once thought dead, would miraculously come back to life. But the arm she held on to grew cold, and his lips turned gray. Zach's struggle was over.

Krista didn't know how long Johnny'd had his hand on her shoulder, but she needed it. She needed him there with her. "How?" she cried. "How am I supposed to do this?"

Johnny sat beside her, pulling her head into his chest. "He's whole again." He stroked her hair like she was a child. "He's healthy and good as new."

"I want proof," she begged into the soft cotton of his shirt.

"Me too," he said into the top of her head. "But we're just going to have to trust that it's true."

We're. It felt like a lifeline.

Chapter Seventeen

ASHBY CRANE WAS snuggled in the corner of Tea and Tennyson, his long legs crossed with Waffles curled up like a fur pillow by his feet as he read a prayer book and sipped hot tea. Ashby required very little in the way of conversation and usually gave only one-word answers. Which might explain why he married Birdalee Mudge. When she barged into the store an hour after him, it was like the temperature went from tepid to scalding. She brought with her the energy of ten suns, and he lived in the light of her presence.

"Scrubbs!" she yelled the minute she stepped across the landing. "Why is your yappy dog sitting with my husband? You know the man is allergic."

Scruggs shrugged, and Ashby answered, "I like the little fellow."

"Oh Lord," Birdie said. "This is not happening. It's like the whole world has gone topsy-turvy." She stood between Ashby in the corner and Scruggs at the counter. "Listen up, you two. There will be no friendship here, you understand? No *cute little doggie* and *ain't you sweet* or I will have your hides." She pointed at him, then swung around and pointed at Ashby. "Y'all hear me?"

Scruggs joined Ashby, and both men increased their doting over the dog, using the exact words she'd just banned.

"I will launch that rat dog like a furry football if y'all keep that up," Birdie threatened.

The only person who seemed concerned in the least was Emma, who had become quite the fan of little Waffles.

Krista whispered to her, "It's all in good fun. Birdie won't stand in the way of someone being kind to the dog."

The whole town had been off-kilter since the storm. Some beach homes were damaged, and trailers were knocked off their foundations, but the Hassells suffered the worst of it. Of course, rumors being what rumors were, everyone was under the impression that Zach had died because of the flood. It took a lot of doing and some very forceful talking at his funeral to convince people that he actually died peacefully in Aunt Alice's downstairs bedroom.

Krista knew the funeral was going to be a disaster, but it was even worse than she imagined. Junie sat in church with her thin ratted hair and low-cut blouse next to her cousin, April, who wore hot pink leggings and whose brother was in prison for killing the mayor's brother. Then there were her alcoholic uncles, all with enormous beer bellies and wearing various iterations of ill-fitting button-downs. One of them, her Uncle Ronnie, even brought his big, black hunting dog.

Embarrassment kept her from getting up and hugging

them, but she was secretly happy they were there. One thing about the Hassell family, they might fight and cuss and butt heads with each other and everybody else, but when tough times came, they hunkered down together like squirrels in a storm. Krista waved at them from the front row, knowing full well that they were all wondering about the tall, well-dressed outsider who sat next to her. She could see the questions on their faces. Had she done something to ruin her chances with Rye Smithson? Had the only good girl in the Hassell family finally fallen off her pedestal and made a mess of things? Maybe she was just like her mama after all, giving away her body for the attention of a man.

She turned away from them, and cut her eyes toward Johnny. He sat militarily upright, his strong jaw set tight and serious, his button-down crisp and tucked in smoothly beneath his form-fitting suit coat. He was inspection-ready. He even smelled good. And he deserved to be in the front row with her and Junie, even if it meant throwing open the floodgates of the gossip pipeline.

When Rye saw them together, he could barely contain his anger. The vein in the center of his forehead grew thick and blue, and he stared a hole into her until she looked at him, just long enough for him to make the face—the one where his nostrils flared, his eyes squinted, and he pursed his lips so tight against his clenched teeth that they turned white. Krista looked away quickly. There was nothing romantic between her and Johnny, of course. They were simply friends who had been through not one but two traumatic experiences together—if you didn't count the wedding.

But she knew that Rye wouldn't see it that way. Even though she had technically *struck out*, he had recently begun texting again. He even called once. He said he was heartbroken about Zach. That Zach had been a little brother to him for a long time. Then he ended it with, "You should be happy that you don't have to take care of him anymore."

Anybody who actually knew Zach could never be happy with his absence, no matter how difficult it had been to take care of him. Plus, it was basic manners to never tell a devastated person to be happy. It served him right to see her with Johnny.

Junie reached over Krista and put her hand on Johnny's knee. Krista got a noseful of alcohol fumes when she spoke. "I'm gonna make a speech," she slurred before waving her arm toward the room of people. "These folks don't got no understanding."

Krista picked up her mother's hand off Johnny's knee. "You're not on the agenda, Mama. You didn't want to say anything. Remember?"

"Well, I do now." Junie stood up, swaying. Guests were still filing into the room, and the din of motion died down quickly as every eye turned to the mother of the deceased.

"Mama! The service hasn't even started yet." Krista stood to run after Junie at the same time as Johnny.

Ashby, who was standing near the steps to the stage, intercepted her. "Hey there, June. How about we have ourselves a seat and get this ceremony started properly."

"I got me something to say," Junie said, lurching for the steps.

Ashby attempted to grab her arm, but she slipped through his fingers like butter. Krista and Johnny stood behind him as Junie marched to the middle of the stage, grabbed hold of the microphone and attempted to talk into it. The sound was off, so she yelled into it instead. "All of y'all comin in here like you and Zachy were best friends. Where the hell have you been, huh? Where in the hell…?"

Krista rushed the stage after the initial "All of y'all." She recognized the tone instantly. Johnny followed her and together, they managed to coerce Junie from the stage and sit her back down. They flanked her, ready to jump to action if she tried to stand again.

Ashby flipped on the microphone and welcomed the crowd. For a moment, things were back on track.

Krista felt Rye's eyes on her. She didn't want to look backward at the crowd and risk seeing his face again, but she felt compelled. She gasped. It seemed like a hundred people piled into the church in the short minutes between Junie's scene and Ashby's welcome. Right there in the third row were some of the most respected people in all of Crickley Creek. The entire Rushton family: Will, Charlotte, Kelly, Allison, Natalie, and Brooke were there. Beside them was Birdie. Scruggs and Emma sat at the back of the church.

Even Jackson and Ruth Marie Buchanan were there—without Virginia, of course.

The funeral got back on track. It was what it was supposed to be—lots of prayer and some nice words about Zach. With each song and piece of scripture, Krista was both pleased and increasingly nervous. She had a letter to read to her brother, and speaking in public was not one of her preferred activities.

When Ashby made her introduction, her whole body went numb. It was like she floated to the stage outside of herself. When her voice bellowed out over the audience, it didn't sound like her own. "Dear Zachy," she began.

A loud, guttural sound came from the front row. Krista had expected Junie to fall into hysterics at some point, so she wasn't too concerned until the splash of vomit hit the church floor. Johnny stood, dabs of bile coating the lower legs of his suit, while Junie melted into the fetal position on the gray industrial-carpeted floor next to the chunky puddle of her stomach contents.

"Mama!" Krista's voice reverberated around the room as she jumped off the stage. It took both her and Johnny to get Junie into standing position. Ashby took the microphone and calmly spoke of how each person handled grief differently. He was on a riff about leaving all judgment to God while every eye in the room was on Junie's semi-limp body being dragged down the aisle. Johnny was doing most of the work of holding Junie up, but Krista held on anyway.

From out of nowhere, Birdie appeared. She grabbed the blue-lined paper from Krista's hand. "I'll finish the talking for you, honey. You just go."

"Thank you," she said, releasing her hold on the letter and shaking her head sadly at Birdie.

"It's all good, sweetheart," Birdie said. "Junie's got a right to be like this."

Krista had a right to collapse, too. She had a right to be angry, a right to be done with her stupid family, a right to be devastated and sad, and a right to run away from the church and Crickley Creek and South Carolina and the entire freaking Earth. She had a right to *feel* things. She did not have to be the good little girl all the time, every day, for the rest of her life. She had a right to more.

But she kept on walking. She made it to the last pew before stepping directly onto something soft and warm. It seeped into the open toes of her shiny black heels and she knew immediately by the smell what it was—a pile of Uncle Ronnie's hunting dog's poop. She shot him a furious look but didn't slow down. She was on a mission to get her mother out of the church, even if it meant tracking sticky brown crap all the way out the front door.

Birdie's voice came through the sound system louder than the announcements in Walmart. "Whoo-eee! It smells worse than an overturned porta-potty in here! Now. I'm gonna read this here letter and every one of you will sit here until I finish. I expect some tears, too." Krista's heart sank.

Birdie reading her heartfelt letter to Zach was not at all what she'd envisioned. She kicked off her poop shoe as she loaded and buckled Junie into the passenger seat of her car. She had a beach towel in her trunk, so she wrapped the shoe in it to deal with later.

"Don't sweat it," Johnny said. "I've been to worse funerals than this."

"I have a hard time believing that," Krista said, her body numb with embarrassment and disappointment. Junie's head hung forward, and her breathing was louder than a bellowing bull. "Thank you for your help. I'll pay for your dry cleaning."

"Don't be ridiculous," Johnny said.

"Can't you see? I am ridiculous." She slammed Junie's door and walked to the driver's side. "I am the most ridiculous person on the planet." She slid into her seat, started the car, and drove away without looking at him.

BACK AT WORK two days after the funeral, Krista felt like she hadn't been there for months. She was desperate for normalcy and needed the distraction of her job. Junie was safely on the couch at her sister's place, and Krista was in the loft above the store. Charlotte had graciously offered it to her after the flood.

It was clear with the first customer at six A.M. that the

funeral was still top of mind and on the lips of most everyone in town. "Good morning, Krista!" a woman carrying a baby in an elaborate scarf said. "Did you get your shoe all cleaned up?" It was a sneaky way of letting her know that even though she hadn't been there, she was well aware of every sordid funeral detail. "I can't imagine who would let a dog into a ceremony like that." The woman knew full well that Krista had been the person in charge.

The day went downhill from there.

Krista was able to shake off the sly and not-so-sly comments until her cousin Kayla walked in. The girl wore work boots and had never been the tea or book type. She wandered around the store, picking up things and complaining loudly about prices until Krista came over to say hello. The girl had the biggest smile on her face when she said, "That funeral was worse than that time Randy got sentenced to prison and Bubba took a piss in the courtroom." She laughed like the memory filled her with pure joy before adding, "All those society-types sitting there in their fancy clothes, expecting something nice. You showed them, didn't you, coz?"

Krista narrowed her eyes. "What are you getting at, Kayla?"

"You got too big for your britches, didn't ya?"

Krista said nothing, she just stared at the greasy-haired girl with whom she shared DNA.

"You think that because you go to online college and you

got you some society friends that you're all that and a bag of chips." Her eyes twinkled with glee as she huffed. "That'll show you." She put down the sordid romance book she was holding and turned to leave. "Once a Hassell, always a Hassell."

It had been a classic Hassell hit-and-run. Just the way they liked it. Spew venom, then leave before the victim could defend themselves. Why on earth couldn't people keep their hateful opinions to themselves? Especially when a person was grieving. Could they not muster up the tiniest bit of compassion? It was like a small segment of society had their heads on swivels and their eyes and ears popping out of their heads on the hunt for any reason to badmouth someone. Maybe it made them feel superior. Maybe it made them feel powerful.

What it really made them was ugly.

People sucked, and she was sick and tired of being the nice little welcome mat everyone stepped on.

Krista was scrubbing down a table like she was removing four coats of old paint when a customer in a colorful Lily Pulitzer shift asked, "What smells so good?"

She snapped out of her anger long enough to breathe. The place smelled like warm yeast and honey. "Oh," she said. "That must be Charlotte. She said she was going to try out some recipes for French pastries."

"My word," said the woman. "They do smell delightful."

The woman was right. The pastries smelled like happiness—like summertime and functional families. Krista should be enjoying it, grateful that Charlotte and Will returned from their honeymoon in time for the funeral. But they were tanned and filled with such happiness, she found it difficult to be around them. Grief kept sweeping over her in waves, and it simply took too much energy to try to match their level of exuberance about life and the future. There were times when her emotional pain was so intense, she shook all over and had to sit down. In an instant she would be dizzy, nauseated, and confused. Grief was like ten shots of pure alcohol infiltrating her brain with no warning. Thank God she had Charlotte's loft. She could run upstairs to hide when it happened.

"Scum bucket!" Birdie yelled from across the room where Ashby's peace and quiet no longer existed. "Get me some of whatever that good-smelling stuff is!"

"It's *craquelin*," Charlotte said from deep within the kitchen.

"Screwball!" Birdie yelled again. "Tell Charlotte to speak English." She smacked her hand on the table, causing tea to splash from Ashby's cup. "Ah, hell. Just get me some of that crack whore or whatever it is."

Ashby cleared his throat.

"Get us both some," she corrected.

A few minutes later, Charlotte came out carrying a plate of what looked like warm, sliced brioche. She went around to everyone in the store, offering them a piece. It was as crunchy as a cracker on top, with soft pockets of citrusy sweetness inside. It was clear it must be added to the menu.

"Here, Krista," Charlotte said, bringing the last piece to the round display table where Krista was busy stacking teapots on top of the major works of Sir Alfred, Lord Tennyson. "You have to try this."

"No, thank you," she said, diligently working on the task at hand. "I'm really not hungry."

"You're wasting away," Charlotte said. "Please. Eat something."

"I can't." She looked up at her boss. "I'm not starving myself, I promise. I just can't eat much right now."

"Girl, you're missing out," Scruggs said, crumbs all over his burgeoning beard.

"I'll take her piece," Birdie shouted.

"That woman can smell the last piece of breakfast bread from fifty miles away," Scruggs said. "Birdalee, you got the nose of a damned grizzly bear."

Emma, who had been listening and quietly savoring her slice of craquelin, spoke up. "Hey, Krista?"

Krista turned toward her cute little coworker and tried to force a smile. Emma was really very nice. Quiet and unobtrusive. Good for Scruggs, too. Poor girl. Didn't she know that nice had no return on investment? It only made a person an easy target.

"I've been memorizing some Tennyson quotes. You know, since I work here and all," Emma said.

The statement caught Charlotte's attention, too.

Emma went on. "Listen. Tennyson, in all his wisdom, said, *Hope smiles from the threshold of the year to come, whispering, 'It will be happier.'*"

Krista shattered like a thin, old lightbulb. What kind of trite platitude was that? A Pollyanna version of *the grass will be green again, your cup will be full again*. It was all a lie. Every emotion Krista had been suppressing came exploding out in one angry torrent all over sweet-faced Emma.

"Stop it!" Krista screamed. "I don't give a crap about Tennyson or hope smiling. Do you see me smiling? *It* will not be happier. *I* will not be happier. Can you get that through your stupid red head? When a person's life is falling apart, the last thing they need is some lame quote!"

Emma burst into tears and ran toward the restroom. Krista was right behind her, but she took a right at the stairs and ran up to the loft. She could barely put the key in the lock through the angry tears blurring her vision. Why had she let herself scream like that? Who even was she? The nice girl or just another cruel Hassell?

Chapter Eighteen

THE SETTING SUN trickled pink, orange, and yellow through the canopy of live oaks and pines. Krista sat at the edge of the marsh near the egg-smelling pluff mud. The cordgrasses, tiny fiddler crabs, and clams had appeared again, but only the stone foundation of her childhood home remained behind her. Her beloved dock was gone. She could sink into the mud like quicksand. Lie down until she sunk so deep that she could no longer breathe. Just like Zach. A mosquito landed on her forearm, and she watched its abdomen fill up with her blood. An end to the pain was what she craved. An end to the loneliness, the emptiness, the vision of her little brother using the last of his strength to blink twice at her.

"Hey there."

She turned. Slowly. Not even a serial killer could scare her now.

"Hi, Johnny."

"You okay?" He sat next to her on a piece of splintered wood freshly ripped from her home.

She considered how to answer. It was the Southern way

to smile and say, *I'm fine*. But she wasn't fine. "No."

They sat in silence for a few minutes, watching a squadron of brown pelicans fly overhead and listening to the cicadas' insistent scratchy screech.

"I don't want to make this about me, but can I tell you something?" he said.

She nodded, still gazing out at the marsh.

He took a deep breath. "Four years ago, I was leading a convoy on a dusty road in the Kabul Province of Afghanistan." He ran his hand across the top of his head and looked out at the swaying grass, presumably not seeing it. "There was a dip in the street—one we couldn't observe from any of our positions. That's where the enemy crawled out and buried an IED. When one of my armored vehicles passed over it, the device detonated." He threw a small rock into the water. "I lost Richard, JJ, Palmer, Miguel, and Reuben that day."

Krista said nothing. For several minutes, they sat with what he'd said. The tide was coming in, and the pluff mud popped in bubbles as the clams opened to filter feed. Each pop became a name to her: Richard. JJ. Palmer. Miguel. Reuben.

"I didn't just come here for Will's wedding," Johnny eventually said. "I came here to heal. I'm staying the whole summer…"

"Why here?" The tiny town of Crickley Creek was not a coveted vacation destination for anyone.

"It's just so different, you know? Back when we were in the army, Will would talk about this place like it was heaven on Earth. When I got the invitation to his wedding, I figured I'd see for myself."

Krista turned to look at him, his military haircut giving him an air of invincibility that didn't correspond with his words or his tone. "And…?"

"I love it," he said. "I feel good here."

She wanted to ask what he did for a living. How it was that he could just leave his job for an entire summer.

He stood and held a hand out to her. "Come on," he said. "Let's go do something fun."

She took his hand and, slipping slightly on the mud, used his steadfast strength not to fall, thereby ending up much closer to him than she'd expected. She looked up at him to say *sorry*, and his eyes were trained on her face. Something in his expression struck her. Something in herself made her rash and impulsive.

She stood on her tiptoes and kissed him.

He responded with a soft force, his arms encircling her, his lips warm and eager. She allowed herself to let go, to feel it, to revel in his nearness, in her need for him. It was shared pain, or shared strength, or maybe just a basic need for connection that made the heat rise along with her heart rate. She'd never been kissed so well.

"I'm sorry," she said, breaking away. He would think she was just like her mother.

He smiled, his eyes crinkling at the corners. "I've been dreaming of this. Don't you dare be sorry."

She relaxed into him for a second before opening her eyes to the spot where her house used to be, where her brother used to live. The loud sound of a Hummer without a muffler made her jump. "Shit," she said in a full panic. "You have to go!" She pushed Johnny away. "That's Rye. I forgot that he can still track me."

Johnny didn't move a muscle. She tried pushing him toward his house. "Please! He can't see us together."

"I'm not afraid of him," Johnny said calmly.

"Well, I am. Please, go home. Run!"

Johnny was expressionless when he said, "I'll hide. For you. But I'm not leaving you alone with him."

"Fine. Just go!"

Johnny walked off toward a huge live oak and stood behind the trunk of it. Krista sat on the wood remnants of her home, back to square one, pretending like her meeting with Johnny never happened.

"Krista!" Rye yelled, hopping down from his truck. "You and I have got some talking to do." He stomped his way down to her.

She turned, acutely aware that Johnny was listening and watching everything. Her heart was in her throat. Rye sat beside her on the spot Johnny had just been.

"I've been doing some thinking," he said. His voice sounded gruff, and he smelled like Jack Daniels. "I put my reputation on the line for you way back when I asked a Hassell to be my girlfriend. So the way I see it, you owe me."

Krista stared straight ahead, praying that what he was about to say wouldn't be too terrible. No matter what, she wasn't going to lose her mind the way she did with Emma, even if Rye deserved it.

"I was not on a date with Miranda Nix, so don't even try to throw that in my face. Understand? *You* are the one who screwed up. And now you show up at your brother's funeral with another man? The whole town was there, and you're sitting up there like little Miss Priss next to some other dude. After all I have done for you?" He repeatedly pointed his finger in her face.

She closed her eyes and braced herself. This was not going to be good.

"I was nothing but good to you. Nothing but good. You hear me? And you purposely tried to make me look bad. I don't appreciate getting texts from my fishing buddies about how my girl has gone off and found herself some city slicker. So, here's what you're gonna do..."

She pleaded to God for Johnny not to hear what Rye was saying.

"You're gonna chase after me. Every time you cry about your brother, you're gonna tell people that you're crying about me. And you're gonna go along with whatever I say about how you're begging to get me back. Got it?"

Krista didn't respond, just kept looking forward. He was

colder and more ruthless than she'd thought. First Miranda, and now this? Unbelievable.

Rye grabbed her by the arm and forced her to turn around. "You owe me," he said. "And this is how you can pay me back."

She heard a crack by the oak tree. "Fine, Rye. Whatever you say. I don't care," she said, praying that if she just agreed with him, he would leave, and Johnny wouldn't come out of the woods.

"No. You see, babe, you *do* care. You care too much. You're heartbroken over me. That's how we're gonna play it. Then if I take you back, it's because I had compassion for you. Because I am a good and forgiving guy."

"Fine." There was not a piece of her that wanted him back in that moment. She hated him. She hated everything about him and his pompous, entitled family. How could she ever have considered marrying him? How did she think for even a minute that he was better than her? He'd treated her like she was a peasant for eight years, and she'd never seen it until now.

"This is a very small thing to ask. You're lucky I'm willing to take you back."

"I said fine." She would end it with him later, when he wasn't so whiskey-enraged.

His face was so close to hers that a droplet of spit landed on her bottom lip. "You will not be near another man again. Ever. Got it?"

She wiped her mouth. "Fine."

"If you say *fine* to me one more time, I'm gonna knock you clear to the other end of the marsh." Every vein in his forehead was engorged, his rage emanating from him like heat.

"I'm just agreeing with you." Her stomach burned with anger.

"I'm telling you, you'll crawl back. And you'll be leaving behind a trail of blood."

She stood up slowly, brushing off the back of her jeans. He hopped up, standing expectantly in front of her, as if she were going to launch herself into his arms like a good, sorry girl.

She squared her shoulders, looked him straight in the eye, and said, "Fine."

A voice from the oak tree boomed loudly over the marsh. "Don't even think about touching her." Johnny ran toward them, a head taller than Rye, a whole person stronger, and trained to kill. He had a deadly serious look on his face. "You touch her, you die."

Rye, his fists clenched, looked from Johnny back to Krista. The color left his face. He spat the word "whore" at her, then stormed off to his truck, sending mud flying as he peeled out and rumbled loudly down the road.

"You okay?" Johnny asked for the second time that evening.

"Yeah, I'm fine." As soon as the word *fine* escaped her

mouth, she couldn't help but laugh. "Why am I laughing? I've lost it." She shook her head, the hilarity passing quickly. "Thank you for stepping in. I probably shouldn't have done that, but he just made me so gosh-darned mad."

He bent over with his hands on his knees, breathing in quietly and exhaling with force. "I need a minute to cool down. I was one second away from teaching that dude a serious lesson."

"I don't think he was actually going to hit me. He never has before."

Johnny nodded, then stood and stretched. "He would have been sorry if he had." He took her hand. "Well, now that that's over, wanna come in for a bite to eat?"

She realized that, for the first time since Zach's death, she was actually hungry. But she couldn't walk into Johnny's house. There were too many memories. Too much pain. "I don't think I can. I'm sorry. It's just too much to go back to where he died right now."

"Gotcha." He squeezed her hand. "I'll take you out."

She looked down at her small hand in his large one. "Maybe we could just eat at my loft? We can stop by the Piggly Wiggly on our way."

A slow smile spread over Johnny's face. "Roger that," he said.

Chapter Nineteen

THEY DROVE SEPARATELY so that Krista wouldn't have to take Johnny home later. She was happy for the time alone in the car. She was nervous. Very nervous. Something about him made her feel too safe, and she didn't know who she would be in those circumstances. She'd never felt safe before.

Tea and Tennyson was closed up tight, lights out, the CLOSED sign hanging in the window. She put her key in the lock while Johnny stood next to her holding three bags of groceries. It smelled like bleach and coffee inside, familiar and comforting.

Everything about Charlotte's cozy loft was much nicer than Krista had ever experienced before. Even in her tiny Myrtle Beach apartment, her furniture, plates, silverware, and glasses all came from the local Goodwill. She loved the place because it was hers alone, but there were no knick-knacks, no matching dining table and chairs, no filled bookshelves, antiques, or unstained cream-colored couch like in Charlotte's. But she had splurged on new sheets and towels, plus a muted pink-and-green floral comforter. It was her favorite, and now it covered the soft queen-sized bed in her new room like it belonged with all of the nicer, better things there.

"You can turn on the TV if you want," she said. "I'll just get things going in here." She wanted to get him out of the kitchen before he noticed her hands shaking as she unpacked the bags.

"I'll help." He deftly pulled out two cans of pinto beans, a bag of round potatoes, and a pound of ground beef.

"I'll get a jar of chowchow." She made it to the walk-in pantry and shook out her hands, taking a deep breath. She had to pull herself together. He was just a man. But he was in her loft. And she might be the stupidest girl in Crickley Creek for bringing him here. What was she doing? She had plans to leave as soon as she saved enough money to get back to Myrtle Beach. There was no room in her life for Johnny Merrick.

She'd chosen to cook meat 'n' three since it was a fool-proof meal. She'd cooked one iteration or another of it her whole life. This time she'd make her grandmother's meat loaf, mama's field peas, fried potatoes, turnip greens, and top it all with the special green tomato, red pepper, and onion relish called chowchow. Johnny had chosen the appetizer, which from what she could tell was an assortment of horrifyingly expensive meats and cheeses. When he pulled out his wallet to pay at the checkout, she was so grateful, she actually got a little wobbly.

"As soon as you get those gold and diamond appetizers on the plate, you need to get out of my kitchen," she said. "There are some secret family recipes about to get made in here."

"I promise I won't pay attention. I just want to help."

"No helping. That's my rule."

"Fine," Johnny said with an intonation that made her giggle. He was making fun of her, and it felt good.

"If you say that word again, I'll have to punch you," she replied.

"Fine," he joked.

She punched him softly on the arm, amazed at how joking about Rye's meanness somehow robbed the memory of its power.

When the food could be left unattended to cook, Krista took off her apron, pulled the tie from her long hair, and joined Johnny in the TV room next to the front bay window. When she didn't sit next to him on the couch, she'd expected him to say something like, "Do I smell?" or "Got something against me?" But he just slid the plate of cheeses, crackers, sliced meats, and olives to the corner of the coffee table in front of her.

She nibbled on a piece of brie. "Know what this cheese needs? Swamp honey." She stood to retrieve some from the pantry. It was her pride and joy—syrupy, not thick, and one of the first things she put in a box before the house fell down. She'd taken it from a hive in a Tupelo tree. "This is the best honey you can get," she said. "Tupelo trees don't have the acid to help them survive in the swamp the way the cypress do, so woodpeckers love to drill into them for bugs. That's when the bees find space to build. If you tried to buy authentic Tupelo honey at the store, it would cost more than I make in a day."

"One of these days you're going to have to teach me about all of these Southern delicacies." He seemed genuinely interested.

"I would, but I probably won't be here much longer." She felt better the minute she said it. It wasn't fair to keep it from him.

"Why?" He snapped to attention.

"Well, I can't take advantage of Charlotte's kindness too much longer. And my mama is barely talking to me now that Zachy's gone. It might be time to go back to Myrtle Beach. Folks there don't judge me 'cause of my people."

"I don't think running from your problems is the answer."

Krista put down the jar of honey. "Well, isn't that the pot calling the kettle black. Seems to me that's exactly what you're doing."

"Totally different," he said.

"Right. Soooo different."

"Hey, we're talking about you here. No need to flip this around to me."

"Fine," she said.

"Fine," he said.

They both smiled.

A car drove by playing bumping loud rap music. In Krista's estimation, the one bad thing about living in downtown Crickley Creek was all the people. She'd rather live alone on the edge of a blackwater swamp.

Johnny seemed pleased with the meal. Maybe it was because at one point in his life, he considered an MRE to be delicious. But the way he would groan with each new bite, reach for seconds as soon as he was done, and repeatedly look her in the eyes when he proclaimed he'd never had food so tasty in his entire life, she was convinced that he was being genuine. For a moment, she forgot her grief and emotional turmoil, and she ate.

For dessert, she whipped up some quick banana pudding, eager to feed Johnny again. There was something immensely satisfying about feeding an appreciative man. This time she allowed him to stay in the kitchen while she cooked.

Her phone in the family room buzzed.

"Want me to get that for you?" he asked.

"Naw, I'll call whoever it is back."

The phone rang again and again. She handed Johnny a bowl of pudding and carried her own while she ran to answer it.

She didn't recognize the number. "Hello?"

"Is this Krista Hassell?"

"Yes."

"Why in the hell did no one tell me that my son died?"

"Daddy?" She plopped onto the couch, spilling some of the yellow contents of her bowl onto the beige Persian rug. She hadn't heard from Earl Hassell in more than ten years. "How do you have my phone number?" She heard a deep sigh on the other end.

"It's not like I haven't been tracking you all these years. Zachary, too."

Her mind spun with unanswered questions, her heart in her throat. "Through Mama?"

"Yup. Up until she got her drawers in a twist and stopped talking to me. Damn woman won't give me a divorce, won't let me see my kids, and didn't even tell me my own son died."

Krista had no words. Junie hadn't let him see them? Johnny sat on the couch, flipping through the muted television channels as if he were trying not to listen.

Krista heard a woman's voice in the background. "Don't you get hot with her now, Earl. You be nice." There was another deep sigh.

"What happened with my son?" Earl asked.

Krista told him the story, but the man should've known his time with his son was limited.

"Earl!" came the woman's voice. "Don't forget to ask about her."

When he spoke, his voice was gruff and deeper, like he

was sad about Zach. “Can I see you?”

“Dad. I’ve been an adult for more than six years now. You could’ve seen me a long time ago.”

“Yeah, well. You know…” He cleared his throat.

“And I work at a coffee shop. You can walk in, order something to drink, and say hi to me just about any time you want.”

“’Cept for that I live in Beaufort now.”

“Yeah.” The excuse was hollow.

She heard the woman’s voice again before Earl repeated what she’d said. “We’d love for you to come over for lunch.”

She didn’t have to go. She could always say no later. “Text me the details.”

“Okay then.”

“Bye, Dad.” She hung up and placed the phone gently on the table beside her. Her eyes stung, but weren’t welling with tears. She felt limp and cold. “Looks like I get to deal with my dad now, too.” She leaned her head back into the cushions.

“Is that good?” Johnny asked.

“I have no idea.”

Chapter Twenty

"I GET MY mean streak from my mama," Birdie chattered to Scruggs over the counter at Tea and Tennyson as if there weren't a store full of people there to listen. "And while we're talking about it, my sass is from Seagram's, and this here body is courtesy of biscuits. Now, get me some coffee so I can have myself a personality."

"Coffee won't help with what you've got going on, Miss Biscuits." Scruggs was already in the process of making her a very caffeinated, very chocolatey, Early Birdie Special.

"Krista," Birdie said, using her finger to motion her in. "We have got to talk."

It took half an hour before Krista was able to take a break. By then, Birdie had chatted it up with almost every person in the room. The locals, that was. All outsiders were pointedly ignored.

"Sit here, child," Birdie said, pointing to a corner table and looking around to make sure everyone else was out of earshot. "Now, we all know that once the funeral is over, people aren't gonna be inclined to give you grace much longer. They're gonna think you're playing the victim if you keep with the sad face. It's awful, I know, but it's the gall-danged truth."

Krista was grateful to sit, no matter what Birdie had to say. It had been an early morning, and she hadn't gotten much sleep the night before. She still owed Emma an apology, and she would have no peace until she did.

"I've been paying special attention to the stories about Virginia and her new man," Birdie said, "and I am sorry to say that she appears to be winning the fight."

Krista sighed. "I can only hope that the truth will win out, I guess."

"Those are sissy words. You have got to fight back." Birdie was leaning in so close that she could smell the coffee on her breath. "Virginia cannot be allowed to spread lies about you in order to get herself out of hot water. I've been doing what I can, but I can't handle it all by myself."

"I don't have the energy to fight the gossip, Birdie. It will pass if we give it enough time." She had too much on her plate to spend time worrying about Virginia Buchanan. "I just want to be left alone."

"Well, alone is exactly what you're gonna be, my dear. And trust me, this is not the passing kind of lie, this is the reputation kind. Just when you were starting to make a good name for yourself in this backward town, all your hard work is going straight down the commode. Your little explosion at Emma didn't help you none, either. I heard a damn bank teller talking about your little temper tantrum. Now—" She pulled a folded piece of paper from her purse and opened it. "I have come up with a plan. You're not gonna like it, but if you follow it, everything will be right as rain."

She wanted to tell Birdie to go away, to mind her own business and stop telling everybody what to do. It felt like she was viciously rubbing salt into an open wound. But the thing about salt was, even though it hurt like the devil, it could actually force bacteria out. Salt could be painful but cleansing. Krista probably ought to listen.

"First, whenever people are around, paste a smile on your face." Birdie demonstrated, her smile toothy and broad despite the seriousness in her eyes. "It doesn't matter how you're feeling on the inside, show 'em that you're stable on the outside.

"Next, stay as far away from freaking North Charleston as possible. I'm talking, don't leave Crickley for anything. At any time. For at least two months. Since you're sad and all, people are gonna be watching real close to see if you run out there to that made-up man."

That wouldn't be a problem for Krista. She had no plans to dress up and visit a far-away grocery store any time soon. And, to Birdie's other point, every Southern girl could muster a fake smile. They were born with that ability.

"And third, you have got to stop canoodling with Will's army buddy. First there was the funeral, then people saw him leaving here late one night. And that is turning what people are already thinking into cement—that you've been cheatin' and that's why Rye broke up with you. Some say that Johnny is the guy you met up with in North Charleston and that you are throwing him in Rye's face for breaking up with you. Just stop with that boy. Got it? You might as well be loading the guns for the gossips every time you see him."

"I am so tired of hearing made-up things about my life," Krista said. "I am not going to change what I do because of someone else's lie. I won't." Screw everyone else. She'd spent her whole life worried about what they were saying about her. Stick a fork in her, she was done.

"That'd be a mistake, dear heart. Don't forget that we're not talking about forever here, we're just talking about now. Oh, and you might also want to tone down the pretty a bit." She reached out and drew circles in the air around Krista's face. "It's only natural for people to want to throw pretty in front of a bus. You get me?"

"I have to get back to work." She scooted backward and stood. "Thank you for caring, Birdie. But I'm not going to play this game anymore."

"I'm right, you know." Birdie raised her drawn-on eyebrows.

"I know you are," she said sadly. She reached down to pet Waffles, who at some point had snuck in and made a bed on Birdie's purse. Waffles's belly was rounder than usual. Probably because Emma had been spoiling her. When Birdie noticed the dog, she nearly popped.

"Scruggs Willingshit the third! Get your rat off my leather bag!"

Scruggs flipped her off, but Emma came running. "Come here, sweet baby," she said as she carefully picked up the sleeping dog. "She's been extra tired lately." The dog barely opened her eyes. "Let's get you comfy outside." She kissed her fuzzy head as she carried her toward the little wooden house and fluffy bed on the back patio. "I'll get you a bowl of fresh cream, okay? Don't listen to that mean old lady."

"Thanks, hon," Scruggs said.

Emma blew him a kiss, and Krista was sure it was Emma who had been feeding the dog too much cream.

"Good Lord," Birdie said to Scruggs. "Y'all are worse than Billy Bob and Angelina. Soon you're gonna start wearing each other's blood around your necks."

Krista followed Emma into the kitchen. "Hey, Emma?"

Emma held a pitcher of cream, her blue eyes locked on Krista's. She looked frightened.

"I owe you a really big apology. I'm so sorry that I yelled at you the other day."

Emma visibly relaxed.

"I am horrible," Krista began.

"It's okay."

"You didn't deserve any of that. You were trying to help."

"Do I want to be a poet?" she said, strangely. "No. Do I want to memorize fun little snippets from the man whose name is on the store where I work? Yes." Her eyes twinkled. "*Theirs not to reason why, theirs but to do and die.*" Emma was clearly quite happy with herself for the Tennyson quote that just came out of her mouth.

It took all Krista had to not start yelling again. "Anyway. I'm sorry, Emma."

"It's okay," she said breezily, walking past Krista to deliver the cream to the dog.

That girl was either dumber than a box of rocks or her mind was a moon orbiting a planet that was not Earth.

Krista had been ignoring the phone stuffed into her back pocket, buzzing for a solid ten minutes. She pulled it out to see what obnoxious person had been texting nonstop. It was Johnny.

"Come join me on Katu"

"I'm out by the oyster beds"

"Near the beach house"

"Seriously. What time are you off work?"

"I just caught a drum bigger than my arm"

"We should eat this fish for dinner"

"These puppies can fight!"

"Get out here!"

No one would see them on Katu. Very few people were allowed on it. Aside from being the home of Jackson, Ruth Marie, and baby Lauren, it was a private nature preserve for all kinds of critters ranging from brown pelicans to loggerhead sea turtles. She desperately needed to get away. She had one more hour at work, then she'd drive straight there.

"Be there by two," she texted back.

"Alright! I'll save some bait for you."

Birdie might be right about staying away from Johnny, but what people didn't know wouldn't hurt. And anyway, Johnny made her feel better. Screw Birdie.

Chapter Twenty-One

KRISTA WAS NO stranger to fly-fishing from the shallows. Even though Johnny said he'd save some bait for her, he was probably using croakers or mullet. She knew the redfish off Katu Island loved blue crab. So she stopped by the creek and threw out a net baited with a chunk of raw chicken. After a few minutes, she had five crabs.

Johnny was easy to spot in the surf. She parked on the dirt road, grabbed her cooler and fishing pole, kicked off her shoes, and waved to him from the beach. His face lit up, and he rushed through the water to get to her. Country music was coming from the phone in his pocket.

"You showed up," he said, clearly delighted.

She opened her cooler for him to see the crabs inside. "Just you wait," she said. "We're about to get us a workout."

"Hoo-rah," he said, pulling a piece of mullet off his hook and throwing it into the water in favor of her crab.

She pierced a crab onto her line, and they waded thigh deep into the water, casting where the waves crested but didn't break, into the sloughs. From the corner of her eye, she studied him. It was the first time they'd both been dressed for the beach—he with his army ball cap and blue swim trunks and she with her hair in a ponytail, wearing cutoff jean shorts and a white bikini top. Sweat glistened on his forehead, just like it did on hers. The heat and humidity would be unbearable if it weren't for the cooler water on their bottom half.

"I'm glad you came. I thought you might be going into Charleston today."

"Why would I go into Charleston?" she said tugging twice on her line.

"To pick up Zach's ashes." He didn't sound the least bit surprised that he had information about her life that she didn't.

"What? How do you know that?" She reeled in slowly.

There was a titch of sassiness in his voice when he answered, "Well, why else you would you go to Charleston?"

If he was teasing her about the rumor, she wasn't having it. "Tell me how you know that Zach's ashes are ready, Johnny."

He paused. "From Ashby. The church works closely with the funeral home."

"Why would Ashby be talking about me?" She stopped reeling in the line, quickly becoming suspicious of the tight-abbed man next to her.

"Well, it was more me talking about you to him."

"And why were you talking to Ashby about me?"

Johnny turned toward her, the tip of his fishing pole in

the water. "Look, this is not something I want anyone else to know, alright?"

She nodded, still miffed about the Charleston comment.

"It's just, you know, I have some effects from the war, and Will thought I should have someone to talk to."

"So, you have PTSD?" She tried to speak plainly, to convey to him that she knew what it was without sounding like she was judging.

"I don't like to put labels on things."

"Well, you have to know what you're dealing with. That's the first step."

He focused on fishing again. "There is nothing wrong with me, okay? I just don't sleep well anymore, and I get intrusive thoughts sometimes."

That was nothing?

"I don't like to say that I need help, because I don't. I just wanted someone to talk to. No one gets it, you know? Aside from Will and Jack."

They cast their lines several more times, no words necessary.

"I guess I'll go get his ashes tomorrow," she said, slowly reeling. Then she decided to tell him. "Birdie said I shouldn't hang out with you. That being with you is like proving to everyone that the rumor Virginia spread about me is true. I mean, Rye and I just broke up. It doesn't make me look good."

A wave came in and broke right at their waists, splashing

upward onto their faces. They simultaneously jumped. Not a second later, there was a strong tug on Krista's line. She reeled enough to lock the line, then leaned back. Something enormous was on the hook.

"You got it?" Johnny asked, poised to help.

"I don't need help," she said, pulling with all of her might. The rod bent precariously.

He pulled his phone out of his pocket and began recording. "That's got to be a bull," he said, just as a fin broke above the water.

It wasn't a redfish. It was a shark.

"Oh shit." They both said at the same time. The line snapped, the sixty-pound monofilament broken by the shark's brute strength. The sudden release sent Krista sprawling backward into the water, her pole captured by a wave. She scrambled to get her footing.

"It's okay," she said. Hopefully, the waves would bring her rod to shore. "He doesn't want us."

Johnny, who had backed up quite a bit, was now splashing toward her.

"Krista! Come on!"

"Stop!" she screamed, just as he got to her. "Don't move! Back up slowly. Don't splash. Give me your rod." He handed it to her as they carefully moved backward toward the shore. The water was up to their thighs when the black-tipped fin appeared again, swimming in circles around them.

"Hold still," she said.

"I'm gonna punch him," he said, still recording the scene.

"Not yet," she said, strangely serene, somehow connected to the beast in the water. The shark bumped its nose directly into her calf. She held perfectly still. "It's the bump and strike." The shark turned, and she cast the line a few feet in front of him, wiggling the crab on the end of Johnny's line.

Still moving backward as quickly as they could without alarming the shark, they watched the beast approach the crab in the murky water, propelling itself ominously closer to them with each bend of its long tail. She danced the crab in the water, and the shark's fin disappeared beneath the surface. With a burst of whitewater and razor-sharp teeth, it took the bait. Immediately, she dropped the pole and they fought the hold of the water as they took off as fast as they could. Her shorter legs couldn't break the surface as easily as his, so he pulled her along until she could run full-out alone.

Once on dry sand, they stared out at the water. Johnny's pole floated away, moving swiftly toward the dark blue depths still attached to the shark. The knowledge that they were safe began to take hold. Soaking wet and buzzing with excitement, she turned to him, his phone unbelievably still in his left hand, still actively recording.

"I'm one lucky Lucy," she said. "You are, too."

IN THE CLEAN white kitchen of Charlotte's beach house, they fried up the redfish Johnny had caught. A simple fish dinner with butter and a side of bread had never tasted so good. Afterward, they sat on the front porch rocking chairs, watching the setting sun reflect off the water where somewhere, a blacktip shark swam with a fishing pole following behind him.

"Sorry, big guy," Krista said aloud.

"You feeling bad about a shark?"

She nodded, and he didn't make fun of her. They both knew that the shark could have caused some serious damage if it wanted to. "If we can outsmart a shark, we surely don't have to listen to the advice of people who don't know what they're talking about."

"Are you talking about Birdie's advice to stay away from me?"

Krista nodded.

"Good." He put down his fork, picked up her hand, and kissed it.

"Sorry that I lost your pole," she said.

"I don't care about the pole. You saved us by doing that. If it wasn't the crab, it was going to be one of us."

"Maybe," she said, astounded that he'd give her so much credit.

"The video I took," he said. "That thing's gonna go viral. You should post it."

She smirked. "I don't do social media."

"How do you keep up with everybody?"

"I don't. There is not one person I want to keep up with."

"Hand me your phone. We'll set up an Instagram for you. You might like getting news, and you learn a lot about people from other areas. You ever been outside of South Carolina?"

"Nope," she said. It was a sore spot for her. She knew, of course, that there was a great big world out there, but she'd never had the money to explore it. Vacations were never in the cards for the Hassell family.

"Stand up," he said, rising and holding his hand out for her. "Please."

She took it and stood.

"Now, I'm gonna put you right about here." He took her by the shoulders and placed her near the front steps, the deep blue ocean and bright orange sky meeting behind her head. "Smile."

"You are not taking my picture!" she protested. "I don't have any makeup left on my face, and my hair is filled with salt and going all over everywhere."

"You look like a beach babe."

"I look like a castaway." Despite protesting, she stayed where he'd placed her.

"Just smile." He smiled first, in a way that said she was the most beautiful person he'd ever seen.

She was used to Rye taking pictures of her, but something felt different about this. It felt more about her and less about him. She smiled, but not for the camera.

"There," he said, showing her a stunningly authentic picture of herself. "The perfect profile picture."

Maybe catching up with the digital times wasn't such a terrible idea after all. "Okay, but we're not using my name."

"Not a problem, Lucky Lucy."

"Lucky Lucy?" She chuckled. Aside from avoiding the jaws of a blacktip, the only thing she'd ever been lucky about was being born on the marsh—sea water and pluff mud ran in her veins.

"Hey, Lucky Lucy?" He put his phone in the pocket of his swim trunks.

"Yeah?" She liked the name. It portended good things.

Entering her personal space, he asked, "Can I kiss you?"

She answered by lifting her chin.

Chapter Twenty-Two

IT WAS SO nice to be able to simply walk down the stairs to work each morning. Krista had gotten used to her leisurely morning without the twenty-minute commute. The only problem was, there were no sounds of cicadas, crickets, or bullfrogs playing their night music, singing her to sleep. She missed waking up to steam on the water and the comforting smell of the marsh. Downtown Crickley Creek was wreaking havoc on her circadian rhythm.

"Mornin', Emma," she said as the perky redhead showed up for work.

"Good morning, Krista," she drawled. "*'Tis a morning pure and sweet.*"

That particular quote wasn't excruciatingly annoying. "Yes, it 'tis."

"I'm not saying someone is waiting outside for you, but you might want to look out the window."

"For me?" It was still dark outside, with only the streetlamps providing a modicum of light. There, on a bench near the courthouse, sat Rye. Her heart sank. He looked up and, seeing her in the lighted interior of the store, jumped up and ran across the street. Emma had locked the door behind her, so Krista unlocked it and reluctantly let him in.

"Hey, babe," he said.

"What are you doing here? It's five thirty in the morning."

"I just..." His eyes were red-rimmed as if he hadn't slept at all. "Mama and Daddy have been fighting. Mama left," he whispered, his eyes on Emma as if to make sure she couldn't hear.

"Your mom *left*?" It seemed so out of character. Valerie Smithson had it too good—she would never risk her money or her reputation by leaving. "Why?"

"She's mad at my dad, I guess. I don't really know." He was still whispering. "She's gone. Packed a bag and left." He wiped at his tired eyes. "I can't get through this alone, babe. I need you back."

"Rye"—she took his hand—"I've moved on. I know it hasn't been that long, but a lot has happened in my life. I don't feel the same way anymore."

"Krista, give me a chance. Please. I promise things will be good. I give you my word. I will treat you like the beautiful princess you are."

She didn't want to be treated like a princess. She wanted to be treated like an equal. "I can be your friend, okay? I can help as a friend. But that's all I can do."

Deep hiccupping sounds came from his diaphragm as a glut of emotion escaped. She'd never seen him cry before. He was like a four-year-old—one minute he was fine and the next minute he was snotty and red-faced. "Please," he begged. "Just one more chance. That's all I'm asking for. I'm sorry for what I said when I was drunk. It's just that I've lost my mama, and I can't lose you, too."

"Rye, you haven't lost me. We're still friends." She did still care for him. She always would. He'd been a part of her life for eight years. They'd grown up together. And, most of the time, he'd been good to her.

"You know about my daddy's brother, right? You know he shot himself all those years ago. I've been having thoughts…" He wiped his runny nose with this shirt and sniffed loudly. "I've been thinking a lot about him and why he did that."

"What are you saying?" she asked.

"Well, with you doing all that studying of psychology and all, I thought maybe you would know."

It was called suicidal ideation, but she didn't want to speak the words.

"Please, babe. Please. I can't live without you," he pleaded.

Ever so slowly, she nodded. She owed it to him. He'd chosen her years ago, and now she needed to return the favor. It wouldn't be forever, it would just be until he was stable. "Okay."

He pulled her into a hug so quickly, it nearly gave her whiplash. "You won't be sorry," he said into her silky, clean hair. “I promise.”

A REGULAR SUMMERTIME-SHORT thundershower turned the sky temporarily black. Customers waited it out inside the store. Even though she was off work, Krista sat reading a book in a comfy corner. She wasn’t here to interact, just to be in the presence of other people. Lately, being alone brought on too much emotion. She missed Zach, and now she missed Johnny, too. He had no idea that she was back together with Rye, and she dreaded telling him.

Thunder rumbled and people milled around, looking out the window every few seconds for an opportunity to run to their vehicles without getting soaked.

She checked the time: three P.M. The funeral home in Charleston closed at five. She still needed to pick up Junie from her cousin’s house, and now they would probably be up against rush-hour traffic. She checked the radar app on her phone to see if the system would soon pass.

A text from Johnny was waiting for her.

“You available today? I’ve got something for you.”

Gifts were something she hadn’t gotten many of. A gift for no reason was unheard of. What could it possibly be?

It didn’t matter. Whatever it was, she couldn’t accept it. Regret and loss made her wish she hadn’t just downed a cinnamon latte. Her stomach burned.

"I'm sorry. I have to pick up Zach's ashes today," she texted back. It hadn't been a full minute since she'd pressed Send when a tall, soaking wet man came lumbering toward her. He had the biggest smile on his face.

Johnny.

"There you are!" He plopped down in the black lounge chair beside her. "I couldn't wait." He pressed some buttons on his phone and pulled up her brand-new Instagram page. "You're going viral."

"What?" Was that the gift he had for her? News of something happening on Instagram? She could not have cared less about going viral, but her heart leapt at the sight of him.

"Look." He pointed to her profile, and she recognized the picture he'd taken of her the night before. "It's been less than one day and you already have fifty thousand views. It's going up by a thousand views every couple of minutes."

She shrugged.

"I knew this would be big." His grin was pleased-with-himself wide. "Isn't it exciting?"

"I don't know," she said. "I'm not sure I want that many people to know about me."

"They don't know who you are. You're Lucky Lucy to them."

"Oh yeah." She watched the video again on his phone and was proud of herself for staying so calm. The shark had been at least five feet long, and watching the fin come at her sent a surge of adrenaline through her all over again. A giggle escaped. "It is kinda cool." Their eyes met in a mutual smile. "Should we put it on YouTube?" she asked. YouTube was the only thing she was familiar with. It felt like the video belonged there.

"Sure. I can help you with that," he said. "You're famous!"

"No, Lucky Lucy is famous. I'm just a backwoods chick sitting here reading a book."

He clearly didn't remember calling her backwoods at the wedding. "What are you reading?"

"One of my favorites," she said, holding up *To Kill a Mockingbird*. "There's something soothing about the rhythm and tone of this book. I can't explain it."

He stood, holding his phone poised for a photo. "Lean back and read it," he said. "Make sure you show the cover."

She grimaced but acquiesced. With each angle, she was more and more embarrassed. It felt like the whole room of people were watching.

"Look," he said, showing her yet another flattering picture of herself. "The camera loves you."

Her heart stopped, even though he'd only said "camera."

"Okay to post it for you?"

"Sure," she said.

"Hey." He sat back down. "You okay?"

"Yeah." She needed to tell him about Rye. The sooner, the better.

"I know it's going to be hard to pick up Zach's ashes," he

said. "You want me to come with you?"

Yes, she wanted to say. "No, I have to pick up my mother."

"Alright." He sat back into the seat, people watching for a moment. "Can I ask you a question?"

Oh, no. Another deep, make-her-cry question.

"Out of all of the beautiful spots in the Lowcountry, what's your favorite?"

That used to be an easy question to answer, but she was still angry with the marsh. She shrugged.

"I heard there's a swamp where you can take out these old wooden boats and go looking for gators," he said.

"Cypress Gardens," she said. "I haven't been there since a field trip in the fourth grade." She needed to tell him that she wasn't single anymore. She needed to tell him now.

The storm had let up and most of the patrons were leaving. Johnny stood to go.

"Cypress Gardens it is. I'll pick you up tomorrow at ten hundred hours."

Because of its downtown business district location, Tea and Tennyson was closed on weekends. The next day was Saturday, so there was only one reason his plan wouldn't work. She just couldn't seem to spit out the word: Rye.

Her lack of answer was enough for Johnny. "I'll bring the bug spray."

"You won't need it," she said. "There aren't any mosquitoes at the swamp."

He looked at her strangely.

"Bladder wort and mosquito fish. They eat the larvae."

"This is going to be awesome," he said.

She was already madly calculating how she was going to cancel their plans before ten the next morning.

Chapter Twenty-Three

IT WAS A painful drive to Charleston to pick up Zach's ashes. A big, white pickup cut her off, causing her mother to scream and her tires to skid sideways. Krista flipped off the driver. Usually, she gave people grace, but she was at the end of her patience: mad at herself for not telling Johnny about Rye, heartbroken to be picking up her beloved Zach in the form of ashes, and if her mother complained about one more thing, she might do more than flip someone the bird.

"She wants me to pay rent," Junie said. "My own cousin. I tell you what—my assistance check won't be going to my damned cousin. Her husband has a good job. He don't need me to pay nothin'."

"Mama. You are not entitled to live at April's house. You do not have a right to eat her food. She does not have to take care of you just because her husband has a job."

"Well then, you need to get me an apartment."

"It's not my job to take care of you either."

"It was your father's job, but he left."

Krista sighed loudly. She'd spent her whole life hearing about how terrible it was that her father left.

"He left me in the goddamned marsh. And not the good marsh like them rich folks live on, he left me on the muddy kind that floods and washes away everything you own."

"Not everything, Mama. Johnny and I saved most of your valuables."

"Well, you didn't save the house, now did you? That was the most valuable. Not that I ever wanted that piece of crap. And the land is in your friggin' father's name. So, what do I have now?"

Krista tried to focus on the road ahead while her mother repeated the same old complaints. There was no way to convince Junie that she was responsible for herself. She'd tried too many times before.

"Diddly squat. That's what." Junie's face was bright red.

The next fifteen minutes felt like two hours of verbal pummeling. Krista was actually relieved to pull up to the funeral home. "Here we are, Mama. Let's go get our boy."

Whereas Junie had been spittin' mad just a second ago, with just as much gusto, she switched to hysterics. Krista held her up as they climbed from the car and walked across the parking lot to the front double doors.

"Shhhh, Mama. We'll get him and then go get ourselves some dinner. Okay?"

Junie nodded, still bawling. It was freezing inside the funeral home, and the instant goose bumps made the place feel creepy. Did it have to be so cold because there were dead bodies piled in a room somewhere?

There was a man wearing an old ball cap talking to the receptionist in front of them. It didn't take long to figure out that things weren't going his way. "Sir, your name is not on the list of next of kin. I'm sorry," said the soft-spoken woman with Marilyn Monroe hair and a face as thin as a possum's.

He leaned over the desk, and the words that came out of his mouth were far too familiar. "You better give me those ashes or you won't know what hit you."

The woman scooted back in her chair.

"That's right. You should be afraid," he said.

"Earl!" Junie yelled, suddenly perfectly capable of standing on her own.

Earl Hassell snapped around. "Stay out of this, Junie." He glanced over at Krista but said nothing. They may have had lunch plans, but he hadn't laid eyes on her since she was fourteen years old. She wondered what he thought.

"Don't even think about telling me what to do," Junie screamed, her vibrating breasts puddled in a lacy bra. "Where in the hell have you been for the last ten years? You didn't even send me money!"

Krista noticed the receptionist sneak off, presumably to get some help.

"I left you with a roof over your head and the car, Junie. You should be grateful!"

Junie flinched. "You are a horrible person, Earl Hassell." Krista hoped Junie wasn't packing her little Colt revolver.

"You didn't just leave me, you left your own children!"

"Let's go, Mama," she said. "They won't let him have Zachy's ashes, and we can come back another day."

Daddy shifted his eyes to her, looking her up and down. "Please tell me you did not turn out like your mother."

His words hit like centerfire. "Yes," she said, gumption filling her up. "I am exactly like her."

Junie stood up taller. "She's going to online college, you asshole. She's working, and she's gonna marry a boy from one of the finest families in town. And you had nothing, *nothing* to do with that."

Had her mother just said all of that like she was proud? Was that what Junie said about her when she wasn't around? And would she still be proud if Krista did not marry Rye?

The receptionist returned with a large, red-nosed man. "Can I help you?" he asked in an authoritative tone.

"The asshole was just leaving," Junie said.

Earl seemed to be considering something. Maybe he had an ounce of self-restraint after all. "I apologize for losing my temper," he said to the man. "My daughter is gonna give me some of them ashes when we meet up for lunch. Ain't ya?"

Krista didn't know how to respond. "Sure."

"See there?" he said. "We alright now. I didn't need all of it. I just needed me a pinch is all." He moved toward the front door like he hadn't just traumatized the poor lady. He stopped at Krista. "I'll text you, sweetheart." He had the audacity to wink at her. "You've got to meet your little sister." The door shut behind him.

Junie's legs suddenly stopped working again.

"It's okay, Mama," Krista said, holding her up. "It doesn't matter if he has another daughter. Nothing he does matters." Inside, she was wondering why he hadn't told her sooner. Why he didn't tell her nicely while they were on the phone. She didn't even know her sister's name.

"You better not have lunch with that man," Junie stated. "And if you give his sorry ass one speck of your brother's ashes, I will whoop you. You hear me? Not one speck."

"Okay, Mama."

"You are my daughter. Not his. He is dead to us."

"Okay, Mama."

"Good. Now let's get us those gall-danged ashes. I'm so hungry, I'm about to eat my own arm." Junie recovered her ability to walk.

Krista signed for the ashes and followed her mother to the car in a daze. She had a sister. No matter what her mother said, or who her father was, she was determined to meet the little girl who also called Earl Daddy. Maybe that little girl would love her as much as Zach did. Maybe that little girl was also trying her best to be good. Her sister's last name might be Hassell, but with some help, it might not be a life sentence.

Chapter Twenty-Four

KRISTA CALLED HER former boss in Myrtle Beach to see if her old job was still available. It didn't pay well, but she loved working with foster children and organizing volunteers. She had to use her brain, and her personality, and at the end of even the worst day, she got to go home to her own place. It didn't matter that the building was avocado green, smelled like smoke, and didn't come with a parking space. The beach was a short walk away, there was a coffee shop nearby, and she felt like she was someone else when she lived there. It might have been too crowded and overwhelming, but at least she felt respected. She'd left Rye for that life before, and she could leave him for it again. It was the only solid plan for her future she could think of.

Her heart sank when her boss said every position was filled. They wanted her back, and would be in touch as soon as a position became available, but the short answer was *no*. Krista would have to start fresh. First things first, she needed to earn enough money to afford a move. That meant getting a second job. Before heading to the swamp, she stopped by Harbinger House, a 1911 Early Classical Revival home. It was on the National Registry of Historic Homes and was one of the few plantations that survived Sherman's March through the South. Krista heard they needed a weekend tour guide, so she stopped by to drop off her résumé.

Sitting at a spindly antique table in the foyer, she filled out an application while a woman in a petticoat with a square of lace on her head made small talk. When the woman saw Krista's name on the form, she snatched up the paper like it was on fire.

"You won't be needing to fill that out, honey," she said.

"I won't?" Krista could hardly believe it. Was she getting the job on the spot?

The woman's sallow face took on a sassy, haughty quality. "We can't have your sort reflecting poorly on our establishment."

Krista stood. "What are you talking about?"

"I happen to be close personal friends with Virginia Buchanan, and I am aware of your, how do I say... transgressions."

"Really. *My* transgressions?" She could hardly believe what she was hearing. "Virginia was the one with a man. Not me."

The woman smirked. "Says a girl with the last name of Hassell."

Anger electrified Krista's body like lightning. "Says a woman wearing a doily on her head." She grabbed her résumé from the table. There was no way she would leave it for the woman to make fun of. It had taken her hours to put together. "You don't even know me," she said. "I happen to be a very nice person, I would be a great tour guide, and instead of using your own mind and giving me a chance, you choose to listen to rumors." She walked through the open front door, her heart thumping like a war drum.

Then she turned around again. "Shame on you."

THERE WAS SOMETHING about the swamp. It was horror movies, romance, and *National Geographic* all rolled into one. Johnny insisted on rowing the boat without her help, and he deftly steered them through the bright green, dainty floating duckweed and around the cypress knees and trees. The black water was perfectly still except for the ripples from their little wooden boat.

"You'll see the baby gators out here in the duckweed," Krista said, adjusting her sundress beneath her knees. "It's what they eat—but not for the greens, they eat it for the little spiders that live in it."

Johnny had never been to a swamp before, and every detail seemed to fascinate him. He was full of questions, and the fact that she had the answers delighted her. "Yes, you can drink the water," she answered. "The oils from the cypress act as preservatives. Things that fall to the bottom don't rot, they just turn black. The water itself is actually clear." She was the teacher, he was the student, and she loved it.

But every time she found herself enjoying his company, she remembered—she wasn't supposed to be here. She was behaving like a cheat and a liar. And if Rye found out, she'd have to take the $235.86 she had left in her bank account and leave right away. The fallout would be unbearable. "Look near the big logs," she said. "The gators dig themselves nests on the bottom. Most of this swamp is just four or five feet deep, but a gator nest can go down thirty."

"There's a whole nest of them?" he asked in a calm voice, seemingly nonplussed by what dangers might be lurking underneath the water. He kept gently rowing.

"Mainly in the winter. In the summertime the male gators can't be near each other or they'll fight." Motion on the shore caught her eye. "There!"

Johnny whipped around in time to see an enormous eight-foot alligator saunter along the walkway through the woods. He threw the oars into the boat and pulled his phone from his back pocket, recording the prehistoric-looking beast.

"Look!" she said, pointing at the water near the gator. "Steer the boat toward that turtle."

He was too busy trying to record the gator to row the boat, so Krista grabbed the oars and brought them closer to shore, closer to the gator.

"You think this is a good idea?"

"I want you to get a good look at this turtle."

Johnny aimed his phone toward a large turtle with yellow streaks on its neck, sunning itself on floating wood.

"He's got a hole in his back. See that?" she said. There was an alligator-tooth sized hole in the hard outer shell of the turtle.

"Alligators can't chew, so they crush. And turtles are their favorite food. This one's shell was strong enough to save him." She looked straight into the camera. "He's a survivor."

"Way to go, little buddy," Johnny said. "Looks like you've been to war and made it home alive." The turtle's narrow head was stretched toward the sun as if there wasn't a worry in the world, and as if there wasn't an alligator walking past him just a few feet away.

Krista smiled. The war reference was very personal to Johnny. It seemed they both had something in common with that turtle. They had been through hard times, and they had survived. They would always have problems, there would always be alligators in their swamp, but that didn't mean they couldn't enjoy the sunshine. Although, in her case, the sunshine would have to come later. Right now, she had to tell Johnny about Rye.

"Can you turn that off, please?" she asked.

Johnny put down his phone.

"I have to tell you something," she began, amazed that the words were actually coming out of her mouth. There was no going back now. "I shouldn't be here with you today. I was going to cancel, but then it was time and you were there waiting and I didn't know how to tell you."

He listened intently.

"I can't date you right now." She paused to make sure he understood. "It's not what I want, but I had to get back together with Rye." She flushed. "See, his mama just left and he's feeling real puny about it." Dipping her hand in the water, she needed the chill to center herself. "He needs me right now. I owe it to him. It will only be for a little while."

Johnny said nothing, just shifted his eyes into the distance, down the smooth, black waters of the swamp. She sat in the uncomfortable silence, feeling weak in so many ways. She never should have come to the swamp with Johnny. It only made things worse.

Several minutes passed before he spoke. "Does he know that it's temporary?"

She hated saying the words. "Not yet."

He nodded.

"I'm sorry," she said. "He's in a lot of pain. For eight years, I never saw him cry. But now...he needs me. I'm trying to be the kind of person who is there for others. I'm trying to be strong and honorable. That's different from being a good little girl. See, I'm not trying to please Rye. I'm trying to be a good person."

Johnny took the oars from her. The large gator slipped into the water up ahead and slinked his way across the top, his tail leaving behind a small side-to-side wake. A small family of intrepid, or stupid, ducks hung out near their nest on the shore, fuzzy babies swimming in a loose circle around their mother. There was danger they seemed completely unaware of, and there was no way to warn them.

Johnny rowed the rickety white boat to the middle of the shiny black water near a cypress tree and pulled out his phone again. It took him some time, typing something in, flipping through pages. How mad at her was he? It was strange to be floating in the middle of a swamp with a man so casually on his phone, ignoring her.

"I think you've got it backward," Johnny finally said. "Maybe the person you need to be there for is yourself. Maybe being a good person is not about setting yourself aside but about honesty. Are you being honest with yourself? Because you're not being honest with him."

So, he was pissed. His accusation raised her hackles, and she was about to bark back, when he put a finger to his lips and said, "Shh. Let go for a minute. Just listen."

From the tiny speaker on his cell phone, the sweetest piano tune broke free. It reverberated off of the black water and the shaded sky and every living thing around them, surrounding them like cave music. It took only a few minutes of bathing in music while floating in the tiny wooden boat, before they were transported by the serenade—lost in their own thoughts and in the eerie symphonic clarity of the tune. There was no one in the world besides Johnny Merrick and Krista Hassell. She wasn't the good girl or the Hassell or the cheater or the liar. She was just Krista. The dynamic of the universe had shifted. Rather than humans noticing swamp life, every living thing noticed them. She looked around, every leaf in every tree brand new in its transformation. More beautiful than just a moment before.

"I'm sorry," she said, interrupting the moment. "I need to go home."

Chapter Twenty-Five

KRISTA PULLED THE green velvet bag from the plastic box and placed it on her kitchen table. It weighed about five pounds, a small amount for such a tall boy. "Hey, Zachy," she said, opening the tie on the top. She was thinking, *I miss you*, but she would cry if she said it out loud. "You probably already know that our dad was at the funeral home." She shook her head, as if he could see her and they were commiserating. "I know you," she said, "and I know you won't mind if I give him some of your ashes. You were always the most forgiving of all of us." Using a long rice spoon, she scooped some of the gray carbon powder into a small mason jar. "I'm going to try to be a family again. We have a sister, Zachy. We have to do this."

Rye was on his way over. Usually, her makeup would be perfectly done, her outfit carefully chosen. But not this day. She pulled her hair into a bun on the top of her head, wore an old high school T-shirt, and left the blue shadows of sleeplessness beneath her eyes uncovered. There was no motivation to dress up for Rye, and her father certainly didn't deserve the effort. She planned to meet Rye in the empty store downstairs. The farther away she could keep him from any bedrooms, the better. Just the thought of kissing him made her cringe.

She locked the door to the loft. How quickly her feelings had changed. She didn't recognize the person she'd been just one month prior. She walked along the black-and-white tiled floor toward the commercial glass front door, where outside colors caught her eye. On the ground in front of the entrance were two dozen roses in assorted pastel colors. She didn't even know that roses came in light purple, muted peach, soft yellow, and ballet pink. Quickly, she opened the door and picked up the heavy vase. If the roses weren't from Rye, she'd better hide them fast.

She grabbed the vase and ran upstairs. Struggling with the key to her loft, she finally got the door open and rushed inside, hiding the arrangement in the coat closet. She pulled the card from the plastic holder just in time to hear Rye announce his arrival downstairs. The card read: *In loving memory of Zachary Hassell. Sincerely, Virginia Buchanan.* Feeling like an idiot, Krista retrieved the vase and set it on the kitchen table. Why on earth was Virginia sending her flowers? The funeral was over.

"You wanna go back inside and get ready?" he asked when she came down the stairs.

"I am ready."

"Don't you wanna look pretty?"

"No." She walked past him and out the door.

Rye was just like he'd always been—driving too fast, tailgating, flipping people off, and proudly singing country songs louder than Luke Combs. Only he didn't sound like Luke Combs, unfortunately. He didn't seem sad at all about his mother leaving. As a matter of fact, he seemed downright pleased with his life. Krista fought with herself, trying to muster some compassion over the hour and a half drive to Beaufort. It was stressful enough that she was going to see her dad and meet her little sister. Having Rye there acting like a teenager added to the anxiety that felt like fire ants in her stomach.

Earl Hassell lived in a small bungalow near Polk Village. It was gray and shabby compared to the neighbors' homes, but the lawn was mowed and there were rocking chairs on the front porch. Krista grabbed the small jar of Zachy's ashes and waited for Rye by the car. In the front window of the house, she saw a little girl's face peek out from beside the curtain. It disappeared as quickly as it had popped up. Then the front door flew open and a tiny, dark-haired girl shot like a bullet down the front steps yelling, "Kwista! Kwista!"

"Hi!" Krista laughed as the full force of a little girl grabbed her around the waist in a vigorous hug. She bent over and hugged her back, taking in the beaming little face staring up at her. "Hey, sweetie!"

"I'm Andy Sue, and you're my sister!" she said with r's that sounded like w's.

"I am!" Krista squatted to Andy Sue's level.

"You have to play with my dollhouse." She grabbed her hand and pulled her inside. They went past plain white walls, free from any sort of artwork, straight to a light green bedroom taken up by a small, unmade bed and hundreds of toys. Rye stayed outside the door while Krista stepped over clothes, stuffed animals, and dolls to get to the little two-level house. Andy Sue already had dolls in hand and was prancing them around the rooms.

"You made it," came a voice from the doorway. She barely remembered her father as anything other than angry, but he appeared calm. Krista's eyes shifted past him to a short, round, dark-haired woman in a red sundress. She was the opposite of Junie.

"You're staying for lunch, yes?" she asked sweetly.

Rye answered for both of them. "Naw, we gotta get back." He'd made it clear in the car that he had no intention of staying, even though Krista told him the express purpose of their trip was for lunch. He said he wasn't in the mood to eat crappy food. They were going to drop off the ashes and leave.

"We'd love to," Krista said. She saw Rye shoot her a hateful look. Dodging toys, she got to the woman and held out her hand. "I'm Krista."

"I'm Laura," she said. "Andy Sue's mother."

"She's adorable," Krista said, noticing that the shadow that shrouded Laura's face was quickly lifting.

"She's a good girl," her dad said. "You were, too, Krista

Marlena."

He gave her an eye-crinkled, closed-mouth smile like a loving dad would to a daughter he actually knew. How dare he. And how dare he use her middle name. She might be visiting him, but she was not ready to forgive him. Especially after his behavior at the funeral home. And she did not appreciate the use of the past tense "were."

Laura put her hand on his arm. "Let's move into the kitchen."

Andy Sue ran ahead of all of them. "One of these days, we'll put something on the walls," Laura said.

The light streamed into the yellow kitchen. It was happy—the opposite of her cluttered, dark kitchen growing up. Laura had made a chicken salad. If Rye's two plates' worth was an indication, it was delicious, but Krista had trouble eating. She was overwhelmed with Andy Sue, her strangely stable daddy, a new woman, and the half jar of her brother's ashes sitting on her father's kitchen counter.

When they'd all finished, Laura elbowed Earl. "Ask her," she said.

Earl cleared his throat. "Alright," he began. "It's like this. See, me and Laura, we've got us some good jobs, and we've got us Andy Sue. We been living here since she was born."

"Five years," Laura added.

"I know you probably don't like me much, even though I been paying on that house you, Junie, and Zachary been living in all these years. But now that it's gone with the flood, I'm about to get me some insurance money."

Laura smiled kindly.

"Here's what I'm talking about now. I need Junie to give me a divorce so that Laura and me can make it official. But damn her, Junie been digging in her heels for years."

Of course he had an ulterior motive. It felt like a trap.

"We wanna be fair," Laura said. Had she noticed the shift?

"I'll give Junie all the insurance money from the house if she'll sign the divorce papers and let me off for the child support I owe," Earl said. He waited for the expected impact, like Krista should jump up and down and thank him. "But I don't wanna give her the land, and I don't think I have to, since it was mine before we got hitched. That woman did nothing but badmouth that property anyway, and it has got to stay in the family." He put an elbow on the table and pointed at Krista. "And I don't want to get no lawyers involved neither. No use our money going to waste with those bloodsuckers."

Krista watched Rye's expression. He wasn't bowing up like he would've been if Earl was being rude.

"I want you to have it." Earl said it to her but looked to Rye as if he would be the one deciding. "Maybe when y'all get married, y'all can build yourself a place out there."

Rye reached over and shook Earl's hand, finally letting go of the frown he'd had in place since she agreed to stay for lunch. "Some damn good fishing off that land," he said.

"How much insurance money did you get?" Krista asked.

Earl's face fell. "Around forty grand."

"Can I see the documents?"

"Now, why would you want to do a thing like that?" His voice grew louder with every word.

"If I have to pitch this plan to Mama, I'm gonna need all the details."

"Yes," Laura answered before Earl could. "Of course." She stood.

No one noticed that Andy Sue had disappeared from the table. She came bouncing back into the room with a well-loved stuffed giraffe, and Earl's face softened. Why? Why did he soften for Andy Sue when he'd been a monster to his first daughter? Maybe it was his age. Or maybe Andy Sue was a better daughter. Krista bit her bottom lip. Earl was giving her the marshland. She wasn't sure she wanted it, but she needed to remember that her daddy wasn't giving it to Laura or Andy Sue or even Junie. He was giving it to *her*.

Andy Sue danced straight toward her. "Here, Kwista." She handed her the giraffe, which was missing an ear. "He wants you."

Krista took the animal and held it to her chest. "He does?"

"He wants to go home with you."

Krista looked to the adults in the room for permission. Laura had just walked in holding paperwork, she gave her the slightest nod and smile.

"Thank you," Krista said, leaning over to give Andy Sue a hug. She held the matted animal to her chest. "I'll take good care of him."

Andy Sue beamed and said again, "You're my sister."

"You're my sister, too," Krista said. The wide, open look on Andy Sue's face, the blind trust, hit Krista like a wrecking ball. Johnny was right. The only way to protect Andy Sue, the only way to help Rye, the only way to truly love her dad again, was to be honest. Just being at their home with Rye was a lie.

Chapter Twenty-Six

"THAT WOMAN IS gonna put me in an early grave," Birdie said, fanning herself. "Flowers? Good Lord, Ginny must be up to something serious."

"I know!" Krista said, handing her a chocolate eclair on a plate. "Have you heard anything new?"

"Not a damn thing." Birdie took a huge bite from the end of the chocolatey confection, then chewed as if thinking deeply. "This must be one of them preemptive strike thing-a-ma-doodles. Something's a-coming." She took another bite while standing at the counter, finishing over half of the bar in a matter of seconds. "I'm gonna have to get that woman on the phone." Birdie took another bite with a perplexed expression.

"Charlotte!" she yelled.

Charlotte put down the stack of books she was loading into a bookshelf and made her way to them. She was still glowing and honey-tanned from her honeymoon. Not even Birdie could cast a pall on her. "What's up, Birdalee?"

"Ginny is back at it again. She's got Krista in her sights. Sent the girl flowers."

Charlotte verified the statement with a glance at Krista. "Was there a card?"

Krista nodded. "They were condolences for Zach."

"After the funeral," Birdie said.

"She's definitely up to something," Charlotte said. "What do you have on her?"

Krista shrugged. "Just that I saw her with a man at the Harris Teeter in North Charleston. But she already threw me under the bus for that one. The gossiping has died down now. She wouldn't want to spark it back up, would she?"

"You don't think it's possible that she's just being nice, do you?" Charlotte asked.

"Oh, come on," Birdie jumped in. "Use your brain. Of all people, Virginia Buchanan knows flower etiquette. That woman would send yellow roses to someone she hated just because she knew that back in the day they stood for infidelity. This is not a case of simply being late. And, if you're suggesting that Ginny is capable of feeling bad for telling lies about our sweet Krista, I can tell you that the woman has not had a kind thought since the third grade." She pushed the remainder of the eclair into her mouth. "She's preparing the way. She's about to spring something on us."

"What kind of something? The man from the Harris Teeter?" Charlotte asked.

"Exactly," Birdie said. "We're about to meet the mystery man, and she's buttering us up." Reveling in her superior detective skills, Birdie was practically buzzing.

"But why bother?" Krista asked.

Birdie puffed up like a turkey in the springtime. "Why? Well, because she spread a rumor to cover her ass, and now she's about to be found out." She tapped a purple fingernail on her temple. "The reason that she sent those flowers to Krista is because Krista was right all along. Sure as sugar. And she doesn't want Krista to retaliate when the truth comes out. See? She's hoping to get in your good graces before we all find out about her Harris Teeter boyfriend. The woman is an expert, that's for danged sure."

Krista wasn't worried about Virginia. The woman was a bother, but Krista had much bigger things to contend with. Plus, the flowers were beautiful. She grabbed a hot ham bun and took her lunch break upstairs. Next to the flowers on the kitchen table was the stuffed giraffe Andy Sue had given her. Together, the two gifts somehow made her feel less lonely. As a matter of fact, she felt a slight glimmer of happiness every time she looked at them. Who cared if Virginia had an ulterior motive? It was nice to have the flowers.

There was a knock at the door. No one ever knocked on the door to the loft. Long ago, she'd taped a sign on the door identifying it as private. Krista answered carefully.

"Hey," Charlotte said. "Sorry to bother you. Johnny just stopped by. He wanted me to give this to you." She handed Krista a note and a small box.

"Thanks," she said, accepting the gift.

Charlotte turned to leave, then stopped for a second.

"He's a really good guy, you know. Will's been in the trenches with him. He knows. And Johnny likes you a lot."

Krista looked down at the gift wrapped in paper and twine. "I like him, too. I just…I can't give him what he wants right now."

"You know," Charlotte ventured. "You don't owe Rye anything."

"Yeah, I know," Krista agreed. "I'm gonna make things right. I'll tell him the truth."

Charlotte nodded. "Well, don't wait too long. If you get used to setting yourself aside, you'll forget who you are."

Krista knew Charlotte was right. Every day she spent with Rye was a day that she lost another piece of herself. She thanked Charlotte again, shut the door, and took her gift to the couch. The note was written on a piece of printer paper, the lines perfectly straight, each letter small and boxy.

KRISTA,

EVERY TIME YOU LOOK AT THIS, REMEMBER THAT YOU ARE A SURVIVOR.

YOU ARE STRONGER THAN YOU THINK YOU ARE.

LOVE, JOHNNY

Inside the box was a little wooden turtle whittled from a piece of pine. On the top of the turtle's shell was a hole.

She pressed it to her lips, then picked up her phone and dialed Johnny's number. It went straight to voicemail.

"Thank you," she said. "I love the turtle. It's one of the

nicest gifts I've ever gotten."

She placed the turtle next to the stuffed giraffe and flowers, and for the first time in weeks, felt full, if only for a moment.

Three hours later, Krista was in the Hummer with Rye. He was taking her to an early dinner, and her head was filled with promises of yellow Carolina barbecue, corn bread, and ripe tomato salad. If there was anything she'd learned from growing up with Junie, it was that when your life was falling apart, sometimes all you really needed was a little bit of sleep and a plate full of good food. It was going to be her last supper with Rye. She would act like a friend, ease him into the truth about her feelings, and let him down carefully after his belly was full.

She listened as he complained that his dad was grumpier than ever without his mother. How his dad was going so far as to have some old friends, who he didn't even like, over to the house just so he could have some conversation. Instead of turning left toward Talitha's BBQ Joint, Rye turned right toward the marsh.

"Where are we going?" she asked.

"Thought we'd stop by the marsh property before the sun sets."

"My marsh property?"

"Yep. I picked us up some sandwiches, and I figured we'd have ourselves a picnic."

Krista swallowed her disappointment. Even with the

breakup looming, she'd been dreaming of the barbecue meal all day. And what if they ran into Johnny? She didn't want him to see her with Rye. Reluctantly, she got out of the truck when he parked. The empty slab was the same, only weeds were quickly growing up around it. Rye slammed his door and exuberantly stomped his way onto the concrete.

"This is gonna be a fine spot for a fishing cabin. As soon as your daddy signs over the land, we'll build us one. We'll take our babies out here and fish the marsh. We'll catch shrimp and crabs. No one will care that this is the ghetto of Crickley Creek if we use it for sport. We can bring our family here every weekend if you want."

Babies? Family? Was he really tossing around those words like he'd never broken her heart? Never listened to lies and then struck her out after three?

"When's Junie gonna give your daddy that divorce?" he asked.

"As soon as he gets the papers all done up."

"I knew she'd do it as soon he started talking money." Rye snorted.

In that moment, Krista knew she couldn't wait any longer. "Rye. Please don't put down my family. We've been through so much lately."

He chuckled as he walked the perimeter of the foundation. "I'm thinking we should build a nice big kitchen over here so that you can look out at the marsh while you're cooking. We'll have ourselves some fine fish fries right here on this spot." He waved his arm like a used car salesman trying to impress her with a clunker.

"Rye."

"I know, I know. I'll stop badmouthing them." He chuckled again. "It's just that they make it so darned easy."

Krista sat on the edge of the concrete where the wooden back stairs used to be. "This is not working." She was sorry, truly sorry, but she was trying to be a new person, and the ruse was impossible to keep.

"What are you talking about?"

"I can't do this, Rye." She looked up at him standing there like an oversized little boy.

"Do what?"

"Date you."

He jumped off the foundation into the weeds. "What in the hell are you talking about?"

"You were right to break up with me. And it's fine if you tell everyone you broke up with me this time, too. I just don't have it in me to pretend."

"Pretend what? Pretend that you love me?" He paced an angry figure eight. "Fuck!" he yelled, kicking a rock into the water. "You can't do this to me, Krista. My mama is gone. I will die if you leave me, too." He knelt in front of her, holding on to her knees. "I mean it. I can't live without you."

"You were the star football player, remember? You are a Smithson. There is nothing you can't do."

"I know that! Damn it." His fists were clenched, and he moved like a robot on the fritz. "I should never have had feelings for someone like you. But shit! I do now. And you are supposed to appreciate that." He pointed a finger in her face, then thought better of it, looking toward the oak tree where Johnny once hid.

"I will always appreciate you, Rye," she said calmly. "You chose me when no one else would. If it weren't for you, I might not be as strong as I am now." She thought of the note and the turtle sitting on her kitchen table. She was a survivor. She was stronger than she thought she was. She reached for his hands. "I'm grateful," she said. "Thank you so much for loving me."

Rye's round face squinched like he was about to cry. "I don't want to lose you."

"You have big things ahead of you. You don't need me."

He thought for a minute and shook his head as if clearing away the emotions. "I already have a hunting lodge. I don't need a fishing cabin."

"That's true." She smiled at him despite her awe of his shallowness.

He looked out at the marsh for a while. Then, as if deciding once and for all that the marsh was beneath him, he said, "Krista?"

"Yeah?"

"You need to know something before you start talking to folks about all this. I don't want people to think that my mama actually left."

"What?"

"Mama didn't really leave us." There was no regret, no shame in his voice.

She repeated the same word. "What?"

"She's in Italy taking cooking classes."

"Oh," Krista said. All she'd done, all she'd given up to try to help him. He'd never been suicidal. His mother hadn't abandoned them. He'd been playing her. She was a fool.

"Rye?"

"Mm-hmm," he said, still righteous in his pain.

"You need to leave."

"What?"

She pointed calmly toward his truck. "I need you to get off my property."

"Anybody else would have done the same thing," he said. "I was helping you."

She extended her arm and pointed harder.

"I only did it so that you could get me back," he said. "To make it easy for you."

"You did it for you, Rye. Not for me."

His face reddened, like he was about to explode, but instead, he announced, "I'm not giving you a ride home."

"Fine," she said.

"This isn't over, you know." He looked to Aunt Alice's place, then back to Krista. "You can't run over to his house and think that nothing bad will come of it." He took a few steps toward his truck, then turned back around. "Get in the truck," he demanded.

"No," she stood her ground.

"I said get in the truck."

She backed up toward the marsh, putting more space between them. "I'm not going with you, Rye."

He stood for a minute, like a bear poised to attack. She held her ground, scrambling to come up with a plan. Then he stepped down, appearing unsure of what to do with a belligerent woman. He hopped into the huge truck, started it with a roar, and rumbled away.

As soon as he turned the corner, Krista sat on the concrete slab facing Aunt Alice's house. That could have gone so much worse. Across the top of Aunt Alice's pink rose hedge, she saw a head pacing back and forth.

Of course Johnny was there. Just in case.

Chapter Twenty-Seven

"HEY." KRISTA WAVED as she walked through the sparse forest of trees. Johnny stood on the back porch stairs, waiting.

"You okay?" he asked as she neared.

"I'm better than okay." Her smile felt real and good for the first time in forever.

"I was eavesdropping," he said flat out. "Wanted to make sure he didn't hurt you. But you had it handled. You didn't need me."

She walked up the stairs to meet him, where he pulled her into a deep hug.

"Thanks for the turtle," she said with her ear against his chest. His heart was racing. Because of her. He kissed the top of her head.

"You wanna come inside?" He took her by the hand. "I bought all the Southern stuff I could find at the Piggly Wiggly. My new mission is to learn the culture here. I've got pimiento cheese, sweet tea, pickled okra…"

"I'm starving," she said. "But just so you know, if you want real Southern food, you've got to go to Tali's."

"Tali's?"

"Yep. Talitha's BBQ Joint." Her mouth watered again at the thought of their slow-cooked ribs in Carolina sauce.

"Roger that. We're going to Tali's." He led her past the kitchen and out the front door to his car. She giggled the whole way.

Satiated in a corner booth, rib bones, tomato parts, and half-eaten yeast rolls littering the table, Krista told Johnny about her dad. She told him about his absence, his anger, and his other daughter, Andy Sue. Surprisingly, none of it made her cry. They were simply facts.

"Andy Sue is just the sweetest thing," Krista said. "And Earl is like a different man around her. Around Laura, too. It's strange to say, because I've only met my little sister once, but I miss her."

He smiled knowingly.

"Why are you smiling like that?" she asked.

"Well"—he laughed—"even though I could barely see straight the first time I met you, I woke up the next morning missing you. I know what that feels like."

"I hope you woke up with a headache the size of Antarctica, too."

"I did, and I deserved it." He reached across the table and took her hand. "Listen, you need to know that I don't usually drink like that. The whole PTSD thing got to me for a while. Being around a crowd—I self-medicated. Just being here, though, I'm doing better."

She believed him. He spoke with such confidence and authority, she couldn't imagine anything untrue ever coming out of his mouth. "Sounds to me like you should whittle a turtle for yourself."

"You saying I'm a survivor, too?"

"Yessir." She reached over and wiped off a small remnant of yellow barbecue sauce from his chin.

His white-toothed smile and deep-rooted warmth softened the direct eye contact he was never afraid to make. "We're stronger than we think we are."

Johnny paid the bill, and Krista followed him around the tightly packed tables toward the front door. They'd almost made it outside when someone grabbed her by the wrist. Hard.

She was forced to twist backward and face her attacker. Rye. Behind him was a table of his friends. She thought he had sandwiches for supper; he wasn't supposed to be at Tali's.

He pulled her toward the back of the restaurant, with Johnny walking calmly behind them. Then the table of Rye's friends stood up and followed them, too.

She dug in her heels when they got to the back door. He was about to take her to the empty street by the dumpsters. She attempted to pull her arm from his grasp. "Stop it, Rye. I'm not going out there."

"The hell you ain't," Rye spat in the redneck slang he spoke when he was drinking. He yanked on her arm. Alcohol and the audience fueled his rage.

Like a flash, Johnny positioned himself next to her. "Let her go," he said with quiet force. "You can talk to her without getting physical."

"Who the hell are you to tell me what I can and can't do, motherfucker! She is *my* woman. She is *mine*." Rye's face was bright red, his lips white with anger. He yanked on her arm again.

"Stop pulling me, Rye. I know how to defend myself." She was prepared to use his own torque to pull herself forward and knee him straight in the soft, unprotected crotch.

"You want to fight me," Johnny said. "You wouldn't hit a girl."

It took Rye a second before he dropped Krista's wrist and pushed Johnny hard in the chest, sending him backward. Johnny remained standing and loudly delivered the rules. "This is between me and him," he said to Rye's group of friends. Then he switched his gaze back to Rye, who was huffing and puffing like a bull. "We're taking this outside."

"No!" Krista screamed. "Y'all are not doing this!"

Neither of the men acknowledged her; they were already out the back door.

Rye swung first, barely missing Johnny's face. From there, Krista couldn't tell what happened. There were smacks and groans, and suddenly Rye was off-kilter. Johnny had his fist cocked for Rye's nose. Instead, he landed it straight in his chest. The blow doubled Rye over, rendering him unable to breathe. One of his buddies moved forward, but Johnny pointed at him.

"No."

The guy did as he was told.

Johnny's hand was hot when he grabbed Krista's. They moved quickly around the building toward his car, glancing back periodically to make sure no one was following them.

"He'll be okay," he finally said after a length of silence and several minutes of driving. They were nearing Tea and Tennyson, and she couldn't remember if they had even braked for stop signs. "I could've killed him," he said.

"But you didn't."

"Yeah." He took his eyes from the road for a second. "Did you see how I knocked the wind out of him?"

She nodded, still filled with a crazy stew of emotions ranging from fear to gratitude to anger to intense attraction. Ever since he'd hit Rye with that echoing thud and freight-train force, she'd had trouble breathing, too.

"I just scared him." Johnny pulled into a parking space in front of the dark building and put the car in park. Krista smiled over at him, and he gently touched her cheek. "You're too good for that guy."

Her chest finally loosened enough for a deep breath. "Thank you." She took his hand and gently kissed his swollen knuckles. "Thank you for sticking up for me. And, thank you for not hurting him."

"Anytime," he said.

"Let's hope this ends it."

Chapter Twenty-Eight

"KRISTA!" BIRDIE YELLED across the room as she swept through the front doors of Tea and Tennyson. "Did your mama sign the papers?" Birdie had no use for tact or for using her inside voice.

"Shhh," Krista warned, coming up from behind the counter. She looked around at the filled store to see whose ears were perking up, then whispered in Birdie's ear, "I don't want the whole town knowing my business."

"Oh, puh-lease. Crickley's been talking about this for a week already." She raised her voice in the form of an announcement. "Junie's finally granting that bum Earl Hassell a divorce."

Several of the clientele actually clapped.

"I heard she's got herself an apartment right here in the downtown," Birdie went on as if her behavior couldn't possibly be causing Krista any embarrassment. "Close enough to walk here every day for breakfast." Her eyes grew as wide as her mouth. "Oh Lordy. Junie Hassell drinking fancy coffee and eating pastries with the rich folks of Crickley. Will she start reading books, too?"

"Don't make fun of my mama, Birdie."

"Alright, alright. Moving along to the next order of business. But first—Scumbucket!" She waved a bright, flowy-sleeved arm toward Scruggs, who nearly jumped out of his apron, caught in the act of tickling Emma between taking orders.

"Get me my usual." She snapped her fingers at him. "Chop, chop, lollipop." It was no matter to Birdie that she was not in line but several other people were.

"Now, Krista." She grabbed the rag that Krista had been using to clean tables and threw it behind the counter, nearly hitting Emma in the process. "Have you been following my plan?"

"I'm working, Birdie. I don't have time for this."

"I happen to know the owner of this establishment." Birdie's smug face filled with gloat. "Now..."

"No, Birdie," Krista said, spinning around to face her. "I'm not doing anything you said to do. I am not pasting a ridiculous smile on my face when I'm sad. And, if I have to go into North Charleston for any reason, I will go into North Charleston. People can say whatever they darn well please. And no, I am not staying away from Johnny Merrick."

Birdie looked like someone hit her in the face with a frying pan. Her cheeks puffed out with the word "Well." Then, she said it again as her eyes darted around the room. "Well." Her eyes stopped suddenly like a radar locked on a target, and a slow smile spread on her formerly frustrated face. Krista turned to look.

Walking into the store on the arm of a much shorter, balding man was Virginia Buchanan.

"Holy cheese and crackers," Birdie said, flapping her arms and fast-waddling over to her old friend. "Ginny!"

Virginia didn't bother to smile, just moved straight to introductions. "Birdalee Crane, I would like to introduce you to Mr. Bob Calloway."

Krista expected her to add, *of the Charleston Calloway family*, or some such thing. But she didn't. As a matter of fact, Virginia Buchanan looked a little…nervous.

Birdie didn't waste any time. "Are you the man who took our Virginia to the Harris Teeter?"

"Among other places, yes," he smiled proudly.

Virginia didn't even flinch.

There was something about him that Krista liked—something sanguine, something at ease with whatever his future might hold.

"And how might you two know each other?" Birdie asked.

"That is none of your business," Virginia said.

"Oh, come on now. Let's tell them our story." He patted her hand, which was holding on to his bent elbow. "She was out in her garden on Legare Street, and I was delivering the mail."

"Wait." Birdie's excitement was clearer than a new pair

of glasses. "Virginia Buchanan. Are you telling me that you're dating your mailman?"

"I am telling you that I am dating Mr. Bob Calloway." The set of her mouth told Birdie to back off.

A crash was heard from behind the counter. Scruggs had dropped a plate.

"Well, I'll be," Birdie said, shaking her head.

Bob continued, "We talked just about every day except for Sundays, of course. I'd bring her leaflets just to have something to deliver. Nothing made my days better than seeing Virginia."

She smiled down at him. "He's an artist. We have a shared love of painting."

He nodded in agreement.

Virginia turned her attention to Krista, who was standing behind Birdie, slack-jawed at the whole scene. "Krista, dear."

She was shocked to be addressed directly. "Yes?"

"Did you get the flowers I sent?"

"Yes, thank you. That was very thoughtful."

"I'm so very sorry," she said, quite loudly. There was a long pause before she quietly added, "about your brother's passing."

"Thank you." Of course she wasn't apologizing for trying to ruin Krista's reputation in order to cover up her own indiscretions. But now, if anyone asked, she could say that she'd apologized. Plenty of people had heard it—the first part of it, anyway. Damage control.

"Well then," Virginia said. "We'd better get going."

"Where are you going?" Birdie wasn't about to let the biggest news in town walk out the door. "You just got here! I am your best friend, and I would like to get to know your new beau."

"Jackson and Ruth Marie are waiting for us on the island for brunch. We have to get there before Lauren goes down for her nap."

"Jackson knows about Bob?"

"Well, he's about to."

Birdie shook her head. After the odd couple left, Birdie turned to Krista. "Well, child, how does vindication feel?"

"Good. Real good." She could hardly wait to tell Johnny. Not only had Virginia Buchanan found a man, but he did not come from old money. Maybe there was hope for the woman after all.

Once Scruggs's roaring laughter died down, everyone simultaneously shut up. With all of the excitement surrounding Virginia's boyfriend, no one had noticed the strange, high-pitched noise coming from outside. Emma and Scruggs both ran full-out to the back patio to check on Waffles.

"Waffles!" Scruggs yelled. Emma gasped as they opened the door.

Krista followed close behind. There, safely on the bed inside her little wooden doghouse, Waffles lay licking a newborn puppy.

"Oh!" Krista said. "Did you know she was pregnant?"

Scruggs was on his hands and knees in front of her. "Waffles, what have you done?"

"I believe it's obvious, Grandpa," Birdie piped up from the open door.

"What other dog?" he exclaimed. "I don't live by any other dogs."

"Listen. I'm not saying I'm right about this, but some people bring their dogs into the shop," Emma pointed out.

Scruggs gently moved Waffles and found two more puppies suckling underneath her. "Look! There's a white one!"

"Winston," Birdie declared. "I'd bet my last dollar that Millie Bell's horny little white poodle is the daddy. That dog would hump a cactus. And Millie takes the danged thing everywhere."

"Waffles," Scruggs said like a disappointed dad. "How could you?"

Krista was thrilled. There was something about new life that made grief lose some of its power. Those teeny puppies, mewing like kittens, were a sign that times were changing. More good things were coming.

Chapter Twenty-Nine

"WHAT'S YOUR FAVORITE kind of ice cream?" Krista asked Andy Sue.

"Banilla."

"Vanilla?"

"Uh-huh. With sprinkles."

"You got it." They were by the Beaufort River, which was actually an estuary, in tiny downtown Beaufort, South Carolina, strolling along the sidewalk with Johnny in tow.

Andy Sue waited impatiently, then insisted on a taste of both Johnny's mint chocolate chip and Krista's Oreo ice cream. When the dessert was completely covering her mouth and the tip of her nose, she looked up at Johnny and said, "You're not the same boy as last time."

"That's right," Krista said. "He's different."

Andy Sue took his large hand in her tiny, sticky one. "I like you."

"I like you, too," he said.

"You're big and strong," she said. "And you're nice and you have ice cream on your chin."

Johnny wiped his chin with the back of his hand.

"My friend Sophie has a boyfriend named Dawson." Her little face beamed up at him and her ulterior motive was abundantly clear.

"Does somebody want Johnny to be her boyfriend?" Krista asked.

Andy Sue vigorously nodded and smiled without even a smidge of embarrassment, still happily holding his hand.

"I want someone to be my girlfriend, too." Johnny said it to Andy Sue, but his eyes drifted up to Krista.

"Is it me?" Andy Sue asked.

"What do you think?"

"I think it's me," she said, dropping his hand and skipping in front of them. She stopped to take another large bite of her ice cream, then walked over and leaned against Johnny's knees. He patted her on the head. But the sweet moment took a turn when Johnny's face went suddenly serious. His eyes darted around like he was in a panic.

"I'll be back," he said with a shaky voice. "You guys keep going. I'll text you." He dropped his ice cream cone in the trash, and literally ran away.

Andy Sue frowned and walked to the trash can, threatening to drop her ice cream in, too. "He doesn't like me."

"Oh, he absolutely likes you." Krista had to think fast. "I think he just really had to go to the bathroom."

She happily accepted that answer and took interest in her ice cream again. They found a bench by the place where the tourists hopped onto extra-long golf carts for their historic downtown tours. Krista looked around for Johnny. Did he really have to go to the bathroom? It sure wasn't like him to run off that way. She tried her best to hide her worry from her little sister. No matter what the adults around her did and what challenges life threw at her, Andy Sue would always be able to count on her big sister.

"Andrea Susan," Krista said. "That is such a beautiful name."

"It's two names," she pointed out. "Kwista is hard for me to say."

"You can call me Kiki. That's what our brother used to call me."

"Zachawy?"

"Yes! I'm so glad you've heard his name. Zachary Earl Hassell. Want me to tell you about him?"

On the bench underneath the oak tree, surrounded by tourists sweating through Forrest Gump T-shirts and cargo shorts, Krista told her little sister stories about their brother. She pulled up pictures on her phone, even taught her their old secret handshake. "I see him in you," she said. "In the way you like people and the way you know how to have fun."

Andy Sue had been such a great audience, Krista returned the favor by watching her do gymnastics on a patch of grass, clapping enthusiastically for every front roll, cartwheel, and attempted high kick. Their ice cream was long gone before Krista finally got a text from Johnny.

"Where are you?"

She answered, *"Across from the sandbar on a bench."*

"Be right there."

When he arrived, he looked like he'd been throwing up. He was pasty and sweaty, his eyes red-rimmed. He didn't stand as tall either, like his stomach hurt. Andy Sue caught sight of him and came running, throwing herself against his legs in a hug.

"You're back!" she yelled.

"I'm so sorry," he said, kneeling down to her level again.

"You must've really had to go poop," she answered brightly. "Watch how high I can kick!"

Johnny sat on the bench and Krista joined him.

"Are you okay?" she asked.

"Yeah, sorry." He watched and clapped for Andy Sue while talking. "Intrusive thoughts. Left over from the war. There were little girls there." He looked away. "I can't talk about it."

"Oh, God. That's horrible."

"Yeah," he said. Wiping his face on his sleeve, he pulled his shoulders back while watching Andy Sue continue her gymnastics show.

Andy Sue came running over to the bench. "Okay, little sister," Krista said, pulling her little sister onto her lap. "Wanna do this again soon?"

"Yep!" She hopped down to run around some more.

"You wanna come, too?" Krista asked Johnny.

He looked unsure.

"Johnny?" She looked him dead in the eyes. "You're not broken. You're a turtle."

"Pretty sure the hole in my shell is infected."

Chapter Thirty

JOHNNY TEXTED KRISTA at four A.M. *"You awake?"*

She texted back when her alarm went off at five. *"I am now. What's up?"*

"You went viral again."

She sighed. The whole social media thing was still largely unknown to her. What was the big deal?

"I'll be there when the shop opens."

That was enough to make her happy. It was strange how she'd gone so quickly from having no respect for him to wanting to spend every moment in his presence. As much as she liked Rye, she had always looked forward to saying goodbye at the end of the night. And she was pretty sure it wasn't because she was a check-all-the-boxes on the online quiz introvert. She'd definitely dodged a bullet by not marrying Rye Smithson.

She texted back a smiley face, then pulled up the Instagram he had created for her. The picture he took of her with salt on her face and beach hair made her look like she lived right there on the dunes, privy to a special relationship with the sun and the moon and the sea. There was a photo of her fishing in the shallows, reading *To Kill a Mockingbird*, and two Instagram reels: the near-miss shark attack and the big gator that ended up as a turtle lesson. The millions of views on those videos couldn't possibly be correct. Johnny had also added a link in her bio to a YouTube account. She clicked on it. There were 3,821,275 views of her shark video in only a couple of weeks. She scrolled through the comments. Most of them were kind: *You go, girl! How did she stay so calm? This video is amazing.* Others called her crazy, accused her of faking it, or sexually harassed her. What had she gotten herself into?

Johnny's first words when he walked into the store were, "Don't freak out."

"Do I look like I'm about to freak out?" she said calmly, flashing him a sweet smile. Somehow, the number of people who had seen her, and even the cruel and disgusting comments, hadn't fazed her. Being called crazy or being accused of lying was something that hurt more coming from people she actually knew and cared about—people who should've known better, like everyone in Crickley Creek.

His face relaxed the moment she smiled. "I was afraid you'd be furious with me."

"Why? You said it would go viral, and it did." She got back to work. The store had to be ready to open by six.

Johnny helped her put all the chairs that had been stacked upside down on the tables back into their spots. "We need to talk about how you can monetize this."

"Monetize it? Like, make money from my videos?"

"Have you read your DMs?"

"I don't even know what DMs are."

"Direct messages. You have a ton. Brand deals, advertising inquiries."

The chair she held slipped from her hands and fell over with a series of *thunks*. She picked it up and plopped herself into it. "I can make money?"

He nodded, pulling up a chair beside her. "I can help you, if you want me to."

She was immediately suspicious. "How do you know about this stuff? I feel like that's weird."

"It's been part of my job for years. A buddy and I started a business—we invented pop-up buildings. Easy to move and set up, fully functioning with Wi-Fi and everything. We sold them to the military and then marketed them to civilians. We've done a lot of online advertising. We use influencers all the time."

She'd never asked what he did after the army, as much as she'd been curious. He'd never offered, so she didn't press.

"I don't tell many people," he said. "When you make the kind of money I have, you have to be careful. I want people to know me for me, not for my success."

"Hold on. What?" Was he saying he was rich? He didn't wear any jewelry. He drove an old Honda Accord. There was nothing about him that indicated he had wealth, aside from flying to Chicago.

"Let's just say, I don't have to work if I don't want to. Plus, my buddy and I could sell at any time. Our company has become valuable."

"Oh." It was a lot to sink in. *Why would someone like him be spending time with her?* She was suddenly nervous and...disappointed.

"What's wrong?"

"I don't know. I guess you're just not who I thought you were."

He looked crestfallen for a moment before his face lit up. "Only you, Lucky Lucy. Only you would be upset that I have money."

She pulled a face at him. "I'm not upset. I have just seen how it can make people mean and high-falutin'. I don't like that."

"Maybe that's why I need you. To keep me grounded."

"Well, according to you, I am about to make me some money, too."

He leaned back, his long legs stretched out like his smile. "Imagine what all those high-falutin' people will think when you're famous."

She put her hand up. "Stop. No. I will not be motivated by revenge. I don't care what they think. I just want to be happy is all. If being happy is getting back at them, then fine. But that's all I want."

"If I keep helping you get the store ready to open, will you have some time to discuss business?"

Krista shuddered with awe that this was her life, then nodded. She was about to discuss business with a successful businessman. *Her* business. What a strange, strange thing to happen.

"HEY, KRISTA!" SCRUGGS said when he showed up for work carrying Waffles and the puppies in a big wooden crate. "Or, should I call you Lucky Lucy?"

She shrugged like she had no idea what he was talking about. Johnny was still there, at the table where they'd spent the past half hour talking about which brand offers were consistent with who she wanted to be online and how much she should charge.

Scruggs placed the dogs by his feet. "Can you babysit for me? You know Mama Waffles. The little white one is Sugar, then there's Flour, Butter, and Maple."

Johnny leaned over and spoke with a high-pitched voice to the puppies. Krista burst into laughter.

"What?" he said.

She could hardly breathe for laughing so hard. "Baby talk. I didn't think you had it in you."

He waved her off, resuming his words of encouragement to the babies in the same high voice. It was the first time she noticed that something was off about him—maybe it was the unusual puffiness underneath his eyes, or the way his face fell immediately after smiling.

"Krista Hassell," Scruggs said, now that his puppies were in good hands. "I about had me a conniption fit when you came across my phone last night. I was like, that's Krista! What?" His hands were moving as fast as his mouth. "You nearly got eaten up by that blacktip. Why in the holy heck did you just stand there? I woulda been running out of that water faster than a moccasin on a lake."

She giggled. "Then you'd be missing a leg now. It'd be in the shark's belly."

"My coworker is famous. Wow." He shook his head, his frat-boy haircut hitting him in the eye with each turn. Pulling his phone from his back pocket, he asked, "Can we take a selfie? I have got to post this. Prove that I know you. Maybe I'll get me some of your fifty thousand followers." He kept going like his mouth had been holding in all the words and the dam just burst. "I'm gonna have to post some fishing pictures now, won't I? Maybe go find a gator. Do you think people would want to watch me go shrimping? One time I saw a hammerhead out by the shrimping pole."

She let Scruggs put an arm around her and snap a photo. Then she smirked at Johnny, who was watching both the puppies and her interaction with Scruggs like a proud father. When her phone rang from a number in Myrtle Beach, she ran upstairs to answer it.

"Hello, this is Krista," she said.

"Krista!" came her old boss's voice. "I have the best news

for you. We just had an associate position open up. You'll be working with the courts to process the cases as they come in. It's a bigger job than before, so it pays more, and we know you'd be great at it."

Krista nearly missed the couch when she went to sit down. "That's great news!" she said.

"I'm so glad you called to check in when you did. It was meant to be, I guess."

"Yes," Krista said. "Absolutely meant to be."

"So, can you start in two weeks?"

"Yes. Yes, of course I can." One way or another, she would. It was the best thing for her. A job that used her brain and her heart, in Myrtle Beach, away from Crickley, away from her mother and Rye. Away from Johnny.

When she went back downstairs, Johnny was gone. Maybe it was for the best. Krista didn't want to tell him her news on a day when he looked like he needed a nap.

The store was packed. A full half of the people who came in mentioned the viral videos. She was definitely garnering more attention than usual. By lunchtime word had reached Birdie. She came into the store with none other than Virginia Buchanan, and neither looked happy.

Virginia sat at the table where Birdie plopped her big red bag, then Birdie strode with purpose to the counter where Krista was working Queenie. "Krista Hassell. I need to have a word with you."

"In a minute, Birdie."

She was not about to wait. "When did you plan to tell me that you are doggone famous? I thought you were my friend. I am hurt. You hear me? I am wounded to my core." Her face was more serious than Krista had ever seen it. It was possible that she might even squeeze out a tear.

Krista poured steamed whole milk into the paper cup she was holding, put a lid on the drink, and called the name of the customer before giving Birdie her attention. "I barely knew about it myself," she said.

Birdie leaned as far as she could across the counter, instantly recovered from her fit of pique, and whispered, "I tried to keep Ginny away. I promise. That woman irks the stew out of me, and I'm sure she's boutta put a big ol' hitch in your giddyup." She nearly hiked herself up off her feet, she was leaning in so far. "You don't have to do what she says. Remember that. You're famous now."

Krista thought of the flowers still upstairs in her loft. She'd changed the water, cut the stems, and kept every one of the beautiful pastel roses alive. But even that beautiful arrangement didn't for a second negate the evil Virginia had perpetrated on her. If Virginia hadn't spread that awful rumor, she and Rye would probably still be together. *If it weren't for Virginia, she might still be planning to marry Rye.* In that instant, all of the hatred she'd held toward Virginia dissipated like fog on a hot day. Thank God Virginia spread that rumor.

As soon as there was a lull in customers, Krista walked

over to the table to say hello.

"Now, child," Virginia began without a greeting. "I'm sure you are aware that you have a responsibility as a citizen of Crickley Creek. I am here to ensure that you do not use your newfound popularity to hurt those of us who have known and accepted your family since before you were born."

"I think you mean barely tolerated," she said. "But I hear what you're saying. I have no plans to call anyone out."

"I trust I have your word on that." Virginia had an uncanny ability to appear powerful when in reality, she was just a prematurely white-haired woman with a huge ego and too much disposable income.

Of course Krista would never purposefully make anyone look bad. "I promise," she said.

"Good. And furthermore, with this new attention you're getting, you must make sure you use it to help the people of Crickley." She looked at Birdie, who made an awkward bug-eyed face that somehow passed as agreement.

"How would you like me to do that?"

"Well, you can tell folks to stay at the Richardson-Steele House when they come to visit. And there's Chaucer's and Talitha's and all of the lovely restaurants in the area."

"Of course," Krista agreed, noting that Virginia had not included Tea and Tennyson on the list.

"And there is a thriving art world here that many people aren't aware of—beginning with Bob Calloway and, of course, myself."

She had finally gotten to the point. Birdie rolled her eyes.

"Bob Calloway lives in Charleston, doesn't he?" Krista asked, knowing full well she was about to rile her up. "Actually, aren't you there, too?"

Virginia's voice grew increasingly loud. "I am talking about the Lowcountry in general." Her right eye twitched. "I trust I do not need to explain how I have spent my entire life in Crickley Creek and raised my family here, and—"

Birdie interjected. "She's just messing with you, Ginny. Right, Krista?" Her expression screamed *shut up*.

"Yes, ma'am."

"Now," Birdie said, "I need you to teach me how to do the Instagram and the YouTube and whatever else it is y'all are using these days. I want to get those notifications, too—the ones that tell me the minute you press that button to put something on the internet."

"You're going to have to ask someone else. I'm still learning." She bit her tongue. She wanted so badly to tell Birdie about her new job, to explain how she was more than some videos and numbers on a screen. Internet fame felt like nothing. She would never understand why people seemed so impressed.

"Scrubby!" Birdie yelled, waving her phone at him. "Come here and put that Instagram thing on my phone."

Scruggs yelled back, "Heck no, Miss Bird. You wreak enough havoc face-to-face. You are not allowed to join any kind of social media."

"Emma!" Birdie yelled.

Emma jumped, splashing coffee onto the floor.

"Where did your boyfriend learn his manners?" Birdie yelled. "I am an old woman and am to be respected. You tell him that."

Emma looked back and forth from Birdie to Scruggs, wide-eyed.

"Fine," Scruggs said, walking over to Birdie. "But this is just for reading. Not for posting or, God forbid, commenting."

"I will just look at things," she agreed. "I will browse." She drew out the word like she used it often. "And maybe just share a little wisdom here or there. Nothing big. Just a teensy little taste of talking to all those interesting people online."

Scruggs shook his head as he pulled up the app. "Way to go, Krista. All these years we kept them away. You just opened freakin' Jumanji."

"I give zero dangs what you think," Birdie said. "Just get me on that app."

"Yes, ma'am." He returned to pressing buttons.

Chapter Thirty-One

JOHNNY SAT OUTSIDE on the bench in front of Tea and Tennyson in a pair of gray sweatpants and a Chicago Cubs T-shirt. It was early, but already too hot and humid for sweatpants, and the back of his dark blue shirt was soaked with sweat. Krista wondered why he wasn't coming inside the air-conditioned store. He'd always barged right in like he owned the place. As soon as she could take a break, she'd check on him.

Fifteen minutes later, he was still there, looking overheated and glum with sweat beading along his hairline. She brought him a large cup of ice water and sat down beside him. He took the cup and held it between his knees.

"Thanks," he said.

It was her turn to ask the question that always seemed to come out of his mouth. "You okay?"

"No," he said, still staring out toward the street.

"You wanna talk about it?"

"No. But for some reason I'm sitting here outside of your place of employment, in a spot where you can clearly see me, so I guess that means I need to tell you."

It wasn't like Johnny to act as if things were outside of his control. "What's wrong?"

He pulled up his T-shirt to wipe the sweat from his forehead, giving Krista a heart-stopping glimpse of his abs. He turned toward her. "You ever have those dreams where you show up late to class or you're naked in the middle of a pep rally?"

"I hate those dreams."

He nodded. "When things get really stressful for me, I have this recurring dream. I'm back in Afghanistan, I have to defend my brothers, and I have no weapon. I've lost it. It is my fault that I can't find my weapon, and people I love are going to die because of it."

"That's horrible." She put her hand on his shoulder. "It's like you're literally unequipped and vulnerable."

"Exactly. I've been having that dream every night." He took a sip of the ice water and hung his head like a beaten dog. "When I start getting that dream, I know I need to change something. That's why I moved here for the summer. That damned dream. And now it's back."

"Do you know what you need to change?"

"That's the problem. I thought I was fixed. I thought I finally put all that anxiety behind me. Then the thing happened in Beaufort with your little sister. And now this. I'm screwed up, Krista." He wiped his eyes to catch the tears before they escaped.

Krista rubbed circles on his sweaty back. "It's going to be

okay," she said, her words sounding hollow to her own ears. "You're stronger than this." She hoped he truly was. He would need to be stronger than even he knew.

He lifted his head and made eye contact with her for the first time, giving her full view of his exhaustion and the fear welling in his eyes along with the tears. His desire to pull her into a hug was palpable. "I'm sweaty," he said.

"I don't care," she put her arms around him and pressed her cheek into the dampness of his face. They stayed that way as she rubbed his back, wishing she could whisper in his ear that they would work on it together, they would find a way to fix him—but that would be a lie. And, not only was she not going to lie anymore, she had to tell him she was leaving.

"You need to go to the beach. You need to lie in the sun, listen to the birds and the waves and the wind. Let the warmth soak into your skin until you can't take it anymore, then cool off in the water. Make sure you wet your head and face, too. Feel it, smell it. It will bring you clarity."

"Come with me," he whispered.

She looked through the window into the store. "I can't. I'm scheduled to close."

He shrunk a little, his head falling into his hands. He stayed that way for just a second, then took a deep breath and lifted his head. "I'll do what you say, Dr. Hassell."

She leaned in to kiss him on the cheek. "You're going to be just fine," she said.

He smiled. "I hope so."

Charlotte came in that afternoon, and Krista knew what she had to do. Even though she was emotionally exhausted, she had to give Charlotte her notice. She had to set all of her feelings aside and do the adult thing, the right thing.

Charlotte was busy packing up the leftover pastries to donate to the local church. She closed the large pink box and turned to Krista. "I'm about to head out. You good?"

"Actually…" Krista hated that the words had to come out of her mouth. "I have to give you my notice."

Charlotte put down the large pink box. "Is everything okay?"

"I got my old job back in Myrtle Beach. Well, I got a promotion, actually."

A smile lit Charlotte's face, and she clapped her hands. "Krista! That's great news!" She hugged her tightly. "I'm so proud of you."

The words were so warm and genuine that for the first time since the phone call, Krista felt good about her choice. After all, guilt and second-guessing were just a natural reaction to change. What she was doing was right. She was moving on with her life. "Thank you," she said. "I'll be out in a week and a half."

"Do you need some help? I can get Will and Johnny out here to move things."

"No," she said. The truth was, everything she owned in the world could fit easily into the trunk of her car. "And please don't say anything. I haven't told Johnny yet."

She picked up the box she'd set down. "Myrtle Beach isn't that far away. And you'll be back to visit, right?"

"Of course! My mama's still here. Oh, and don't tell her, either. Just don't tell anyone. Okay?"

"You got it. I can always fill in until we find someone to take your spot. Just let me know when it's safe to start looking."

"It'll be soon, I promise. Just a day or two."

Charlotte gave her a thumbs-up and unlocked the front door. "Poor Johnny," she said on the way out. "He's going to be heartbroken."

As soon as Charlotte left, Krista ran upstairs. Heartbroken? She might be right. And, he needed her now. But he'd only rented Aunt Alice's house for the summer. The truth was, she had no idea what his future plans were or how she would fit into them. A girl couldn't give up her whole future for a guy who wasn't staying. She had to keep telling herself that, because her impending move was starting to feel real. The sharp pangs of heartbreak were hers.

She texted Johnny. *"Are you at the beach?"*

She didn't receive a reply.

That fact messed with her head. When what she craved was stability, when she'd been fighting to feel worthy, and was just beginning to feel good enough, she needed Johnny to respond.

She texted again. *"Where are you?"*

Her lunch dishes sat dirty in the kitchen sink. She set about cleaning them, observing with renewed clarity that almost nothing in the loft was hers—not even the scrubber she used to rub off the stuck-on food. Placing the dishes in the dishwasher, she opened the pantry door, feeling a need to see something she owned. Something she loved. Two jars of chowchow and a jar of Tupelo honey sat by a box of All-Bran and a can of garbanzo beans. The mason jars were at least ten years old and had been used over and over again for whatever it was Junie had been canning at the time.

As proud as she'd been about her Tupelo honey before, it now looked sorrier than a rotted possum carcass. Like she'd brought trash in from the side of the road. The floral comforter she'd splurged on, the one she'd loved so much, suddenly looked childish. It was like she had nothing to show for her entire life. Everything that mattered belonged to someone else.

She felt like an impostor. Who did she think she was, trying to fit in with normal people? And how stupid was she to think she could ever win over a man like Johnny?

She plopped into a seat at the kitchen table and stared straight ahead, her eyes eventually dropping to her gifts in the center. She picked up the wooden turtle, cupping it in her hand. Then she reached for the stuffed giraffe and held both treasures to her chest. It was time to silence the voice in her head that kept telling her she wasn't enough. She was worthy of love. She was worthy of acceptance. And she would tell herself that every day until she believed it.

She tried texting Johnny again. *"Is everything okay?"*

There was no answer.

Chapter Thirty-Two

SCRUGGS LOOKED LIKE the Hunchback of Notre Dame dragging himself and his crate full of puppies into Tea and Tennyson that morning. Emma had called in sick for the entire week. She stopped answering his phone calls and texts. He had no idea why.

Scruggs looked like Krista felt. What a pair they made, moving through the motions of their jobs like zombies. Neither of them needed to speak a word, their mutual upsets and worries somehow connecting them in a partnership. They shared duties like an old married couple, taking turns checking on the puppies on the back patio and servicing the customers up front. Krista was holding Sugar, the tiny white one with a curled-up tail and little black nose, when Johnny tracked her down outside. She hadn't heard from him in three confusing, disappointing, hot and cold, up and down days.

"Hey," he said. "I'm so sorry. I just got your texts."

Her body betrayed her as every nerve ending tingled with his presence. She didn't acknowledge him, just sat down, pulling Sugar onto her lap.

"I'm really sorry. I never should have disappeared like that. Can I explain something to you?"

The puppy mewed like a kitten, and she kissed her soft head. She was angry. What could he possibly say to account for three days of ignoring her? She shrugged, not a speck of a smile on her face.

"You've heard of General Patton, right?"

She nodded.

"He was a hard-ass leader. And he was the guy who said that fatigue makes cowards of us all." He looked around, then squatted in front of her. "I'm human, Krista. I got worn down, and I started acting like a coward. I had to get control of my sleep and my thoughts. I had to fix it."

"Are you sleeping now?" She already knew the answer. She could tell just by looking at him. He wasn't puffy anymore, and there was color in his face.

"I am. It took a while. I had to get disciplined with myself."

She wanted to know what that meant. But she was leaving, and the last thing she wanted to do was to get into a conversation with Johnny that might make her like him more. She had been working for three days to try and like him less. "Good for you," she said.

"Listen, Ashby gave me some homework," he said. "If you're willing to join me, I thought we might do it together."

Sugar kept trying to crawl off of Krista's lap. It was like

the puppy was desperate to get to Johnny. "I have to get back to work," she said, handing him the puppy.

"Join me if you can," he said, following her inside. He stationed himself in a corner with the newly calm puppy in one arm and the ringed binder he'd been carrying on the table. Out of the corner of her eye, she watched him pull a pen from his back pocket and start writing. Journaling? The last thing she wanted to do was put her feelings down on paper. It was hard enough to deal with them as thoughts. Making them real and permanent, available for others to read, was out of the question. There was still too much to accept, to make sense of.

Birdie's arrival was actually a welcome relief.

Birdie marched straight to her favorite nemesis. "Don't think I'm gonna baby you now that you got your heart broken," she said to Scruggs.

He ignored her.

"Hellooooo? Scrawny? She might come back, you know. She might really be sick."

No answer.

"Scruffy?"

He did not acknowledge her at all.

"Freakin' Scruggly Uncookedham the third? Are you listening to me?"

Krista, and probably Johnny, knew he could hear every word.

"What you need is to stop focusing on yourself and start

focusing on others. That's how you get to feelin' better," Birdie announced. "You can start by fixing me a drink."

Scruggs didn't put up a fight, he just obediently began putting together her signature coffee creation.

Birdie sidled up to Krista. "Ain't much to do in here right now. I'm the only customer aside from that incredibly handsome man sitting over there holding a puppy like one of them firefighters in a fundraising calendar. Poor guy needs some companionship, and he don't want it from me."

"I am aware," Krista said, walking away.

"Don't mess with me, Krista Hassell." Birdie hustled to keep up. "What is going on? I thought you two were hitting it off something special."

She put a finger up to her lips to quiet Birdie, then shrugged.

Birdie shrugged in sassy, sarcastic imitation. "You gettin' cold feet?"

"Shhhhh," Krista tried again, cutting her hand across her neck in the universal sign to stop immediately.

"Johnny!" Birdie yelled, throwing a satisfied grin at Krista.

Johnny looked up from his writing, and Krista wanted to sucker punch Birdie in the gut.

"Young man, what did you do to my girl? Why is she acting like she's mute?"

"It looks to me like she's trying to work," he said.

"Go sit with the man," Birdie said, pushing Krista toward Johnny's table.

"Birdie!" Krista squirmed away from her. "I am doing my job."

"I hear you won't be doing it much longer."

Krista stopped in her tracks.

"Your mama told me."

"Birdie, please." Krista cut her eyes toward Johnny in a way that only Birdie could see. Then she fast-walked toward the back stairs to get out of his line of sight.

"Please what?" It took her a few blinks until she followed Krista like a lost child. "He doesn't know?" she whispered.

Krista shook her head.

"Oh, sheesh, girl. You best get on that. Bad news only gets worse with time."

"I know." She left Birdie to jump back behind the counter. A rowdy group of high schoolers had just entered and would certainly be ordering several of the sweetest, most complicated drinks.

The phone in her apron pocket buzzed when she was down to the last out of the six multi-ingredient blended drinks. It was a text from Johnny.

"I have to go. I left something on the table for you."

She looked up in time to see him waving goodbye at her. She waved back sadly, wishing she hadn't missed her chance to sit with him. She still didn't understand why he'd been absent and then suddenly reappeared.

When she finally came out from behind the counter,

Birdie had a piece of paper in her hand. "I know what this is," she said, somewhat subdued now that Johnny was gone. "Sometimes my husband has people do this when they need help figuring out their purpose."

She handed the paper to Krista. At the top in block-lettered manuscript, it said, EULOGY FOR KRISTA HASSELL. Johnny had written a paragraph beneath it.

"Eulogy? Like the speech he's gonna make at my funeral?"

"That's right," Birdie said. "It's not your résumé, and it's not your obituary, it's what people are gonna say about you when you're gone."

"I'm not planning to die anytime soon," she said.

"Stop trying to miss the point, dear heart."

Krista completely understood. She just didn't want to think about it.

Chapter Thirty-Three

KRISTA WAS HAVING a hard time getting used to spending nights alone. She wrapped herself in Charlotte's knit blanket on the couch and flipped through the cable channels. It was too quiet and empty in the loft. She missed sitting on the back porch with Zach and Junie, listening to the sounds of the marsh, surrounded by night critters crawling out from their hiding spots. She missed Zach's warm body in the bed next to her and the sound of rainfall on the tin roof. She even missed Rye and the way she felt when they were out together, proud to be his girlfriend, grateful that at least one person had chosen her. And she missed Johnny. She missed feeling hopeful.

Strangely, the last part made her sadder than the first two thoughts. Yes, she missed her old house on the marsh, she sorely missed her little brother, but for her hope to come from a man? That was pitiful. She felt the fight in her core begin to kick in. What had Birdie said about that piece of paper? That it would help a person find their purpose? She threw off the blanket and ran downstairs. In the store, lit by the moon outside, she found the piece of paper sitting on a table near the stairs.

Eulogy for Krista Hassell

I wish the whole world could know Krista Hassell. Actually, I wish Krista Hassell could know Krista Hassell. She never understood how special she was. How different. How rare. Held down by the jealousy and conceit of others, she died before she knew her value. and sadly, hers was greater than most. Anyone who has studied human behavior, like Krista, knows that compassion is learned, and hard times build character. Krista had both–the hardships she endured created a person who understood deeply the pain of others–yet expected too much of herself. So much so, that she never realized how much she had to offer, how smart, how resilient, how insightful she was. How beautiful she was in her imperfection.

Don't remember Krista for what she didn't have, because none of that was important. Remember her for this: Every word he wrote in his perfect all caps resonated with her like a hard-fought truth. But it sat in her chest like regret. He left off in the spot she wanted him to finish most. What did she want to be remembered for? Who was she, really?

The grumbling of a truck outside caught her attention. She didn't have to look. She knew it was Rye, probably a few beers in on a Friday night, driving by to send a message to his ex-girlfriend. What that message was, she had no idea. Was he angry or devastated? He'd been both, and she wasn't sure which one would stick. She didn't look out the window, having no desire to lay eyes on his red Hummer ever again. Or at least for a very long time.

Instead, she pulled up her Instagram app. She didn't often look at it without Johnny. It took some time to figure it out, but after some trying, she was able to search for Rye. He'd been using the app for years, and a picture of him from his junior year in high school popped up quickly. He was in his football uniform, celebrating a victory, pumped up and on top of the world. She could see his posts without "following" him, so she scrolled through all of them. It took almost an hour. There was not one picture of her in all of the hundreds of pictures he'd posted over the years. But there were pictures of every popular girl in her high school, most of whom had been horrible to her. The last two photos, the ones from just a few days ago, were of Rye and Miranda.

She felt like an idiot. She'd been so resistant to social media that Rye was able to keep her in the dark. No wonder he was so upset when she went viral. She had power now. She had just jumped into his arena.

It was time to talk to Johnny. Time to ask questions and time to tell him the truth.

She pulled her hair into a ponytail, threw on her navy-blue sundress, and applied lip gloss. She locked the door to Tea and Tennyson behind her as she ran to her car, her heart beating faster than hummingbird wings. Johnny had been right about the eulogy. He'd been right about so much. She was, as he'd said, different. Maybe that was a good thing. She certainly didn't want to be like the crowd she'd known in high school. But she wasn't going to give up her new confidence for him. She was good enough, worthy enough, strong enough, to be alone.

Instead of going straight to Johnny's place, she pulled into her property, rolled down her windows so she could smell the pluff mud, and stared at the eulogy. She should probably fill it in before she saw him, have her thoughts fleshed out, and put some effort into the assignment. There was just enough light from the moon to see the page. The familiar sounds and smells got her in a reflective mood, and soon she was imagining herself laid out in a coffin in front of the people who cared about her most: Junie, Birdie, Charlotte, Scruggs, Earl, Laura, and Andy Sue. Some of the people in the audience would only be there to be seen, and most of her family would show up because they felt it was their duty, or to eat the casseroles and cakes in the church basement afterward.

But there was a fourth category of people: the ones she didn't know yet. The ones who didn't know her name—the people she would meet in her future. To those people, she could be someone better. She could be the kind of person who brought them happiness, who made a difference in their lives. That was who she wanted to be. But how?

She could tell by the smell that an evening storm was on its way. She rolled up her windows and leaned her head back. When she closed her eyes, Zachy came to mind. She imagined him holding a fishing pole at the end of their old dock, laughing like he used to, his big guffaw, daring the fish to take the bait. Why was she still here when he wasn't? Even though he was younger, he'd always been the wise one, the one who learned through observation, who saw things for what they were and still managed to be genuinely grateful and happy. How could she be more like him?

"Hey," came a deep voice from very near her car.

She jumped. "You scared the pee out of me!"

"Sorry," Johnny said. "I saw you sitting here and wanted to make sure everything's alright."

"You're always checking on me," she said. "I'm fine. I was just thinking."

His eyes went to the eulogy and pen on her lap. "Wanna go for a walk?" he asked.

She nodded and rolled up the window before he opened the door for her. "There's a storm coming," she said, leaving the pen and paper on the seat. "You never know how bad these things will be."

Krista and Johnny walked along the shoreline. He tried to hold her hand, but she refused. "I have things I need to say," she began.

"Me, too." They were heading in the direction of his rental. She hadn't noticed until they were right up on it, but the missing part of his dock had fresh wood all the way out to the depths. "Hey!" she said. "Your dock is fixed."

"It's one of the things I did while I put away my phone. I should've told you what I was doing, but I wasn't really sure myself." They walked to the end of the long wooden structure just in time for the sky to release huge droplets of warm rain. "It wasn't easy. It was like my brain was a cave that I blindly ventured deep inside. Alone. I had to be alone."

With her hair plastered to her head and the moon acting as their personal spotlight, she turned to him and smiled.

"I should've told you," he said. "But it was like instinct took over, like my body knew what I had to do. I had to listen to it, and that meant total focus. I didn't even purposefully set my phone aside; I just didn't come back to it. I hauled wood, I slept, I ate, I sawed, I nailed, I prayed, I swam, and I thought about you a lot."

Krista knew how the marsh worked. She'd forgiven him the moment she saw the reconstructed dock. Reaching for his hand, she looked up at him. "Is my mascara smeared?"

He laughed, and rubbed a thumb underneath her eyes. "There you go." He moved his other hand to her face. "Krista. I'm sorry. I won't ever do that again."

She took his hand and kissed it, looking out over the soggy marsh alive with thousands of tiny splashes as the rain hit the surface. She was amazed that she believed him. "I understand."

Johnny hugged her so tightly that her feet raised from the ground. When he put her back down, he actually seemed a little nervous. He ran his hand through his soaked hair and stared up at Aunt Alice's house.

"Remember when your brother was dying?" he asked.

She nodded. She would never forget, of course.

"I promised him that I would watch over you and Junie." He wiped the rain from his eyes and focused on her face. "And I can't do that from Chicago."

Her eyes popped wide open. "What?"

"When I said I needed to change something? I figured out what it was."

"Johnny." The word came out like a breath.

"I bought this place," he said. "I'm staying."

Krista felt the shock shoot down to her toes. The tabby house on the hill, the one she'd grown up thinking was the most beautiful, the best house on the marsh, belonged to Johnny? Even in the rain, it was the perfect mix of historically beautiful, sturdy, and safe. Lightning struck with a flash and a crack out over the water. She jumped. Thunder followed immediately after. Johnny grabbed her hand.

"It's not safe to be out here," he said.

"No kidding!" She was already pulling him through the rain toward Aunt—no, toward *Johnny's* house. Another bolt temporarily blinded her as it struck something on the ground on the far side of her property. It produced a shower of sparks. "What was that?!" she yelled as she approached the garden.

Johnny swung open the gate and ushered her through. "Something metal! Get inside!"

They dripped onto the kitchen floor, soaked to the bone and laughing. "The big guy in the sky isn't happy you're staying," she said.

"Are you happy?" He moved the hair that was plastered onto the side of her face, then put his arms around her waist.

She took a deep breath. "I am very happy you're staying."

He bent down and kissed her sweetly. A drop from his hair landed square on her nose. "I'll get us some towels," he said, heading into the room where Zach had died.

She stood in the kitchen feeling sad and exhilarated and nervous, but mostly happy. She didn't want to tell him that she was moving to Myrtle Beach. She didn't want to be near the room where her brother died. But Johnny was *staying*. For *her*.

He tossed a towel to her. "Here ya go." They both patted themselves as dry as possible, but her navy-blue dress was still stuck to her. "Want to borrow a T-shirt?"

"Yes, please."

He ran up the stairs to the master bedroom and came back down quickly. He had changed into a plain white T-shirt and held his gray army shirt in his hand. "This okay?"

"Perfect." She took it into the bathroom and tugged off her outfit. The shirt was so big that it fell to mid-thigh and fit her like a minidress. She took some toilet paper and wiped the shadow of mascara from under her eyes, then finger-brushed her hair. That was as good as it was going to get.

When she entered the kitchen, Johnny had set out a bowl of pimiento cheese and a box of butter crackers. "What can I get you to drink?"

"Just water is fine," she said, suddenly so jittery that she could barely speak.

When he looked at her, really looked at her, he stopped what he was doing. It was as if he'd just noticed her standing in his kitchen, wearing his T-shirt, and it took his breath away. She took a step back. "I, uh," she said. "I'm leaving."

He snapped back to where he'd been the moment before. "Don't leave yet. I just put out the cheese." He laughed and pretended to pout.

"No. I mean, I'm leaving Crickley. I got a job in Myrtle Beach." She felt like she did when she'd told Zach that she was leaving the first time. Like she was making a mistake. Like she was about to miss out on something important. She held her breath waiting for his reaction.

Johnny leaned against the small kitchen island. "When are you leaving?"

She nodded. "Next Saturday. A week from tomorrow."

Johnny walked past her into the family room. He sat in his easy chair and looked out the window. "The storm is passing."

"That's what they do out here. They pop in and out." Her voice didn't sound normal. It was soft and wary.

"What do you think that lightning hit?" he asked.

She shrugged.

"Want to go look?"

She looked down at her T-shirt outfit. "I think we should talk about this first."

"You're right," he said. "We should." He stood and walked to the back door where he slipped on his flip-flops. "There's that space, you know. That space between stimulus and response. I need a little extra space right now. Just for a couple of minutes." He opened the door and stepped outside. "You stay here. I'm going to go check out what the lightning hit."

Krista took a seat in the kitchen where she could look out the back window. She watched Johnny sprint across her property, then veer off toward an overgrown area filled with palmettos. He disappeared behind the greenery for several minutes, then came marching out. She couldn't see his face, but she hoped he'd found what he was looking for. He took his time walking back. By the time he walked up the steps to the back door, Krista was tired of waiting. She wanted to get the conversation over with. Whatever reaction he was going to have, she was ready for it.

"It's your old bathtub," he announced, kicking off his shoes.

She sat straight up. "The old iron one?" She'd taken countless cold rust-colored baths in that old beast. She'd bathed her little brother in it, tried to sober up her mother in it. She'd sat in that tub when she had a high fever and escaped to it when she needed some time alone. She didn't realize until she looked up at Johnny that tears were streaming down her face.

"You okay?" It was his usual question, like he was always taking her temperature, always making sure she was stable, hoping she was happy.

"I'm glad you found it," she said. "Is it still in one piece?"

"Looks to be." He pulled out a chair and sat next to her, reaching for her hand. "I'm proud of you for landing that job. I want to hear all about it. Myrtle Beach is not that far away. We can make this work."

The last thing she wanted was another long-distance relationship. She'd done that with Rye, and she had no desire to do it again. But she needed more time to think. This was not Rye, it was Johnny. Plus, there was something about that stupid old tub that felt like a sign.

"I'm not giving up on you, Krista Hassell." He squeezed her hand then leaned in and kissed her like he didn't see her ruined makeup and her frizzy hair. Like he wasn't mad that she moved forward without him. Like he would always give her space to grow.

Chapter Thirty-Four

KRISTA SAT AT the kitchen table in the loft, the eulogy in front of her. She couldn't sleep, so she was up before the sun. She read every word Johnny had written at the top several times, hoping to gain inspiration. Then it occurred to her—hadn't Johnny written his own? Why had she never asked to see it? It had been his idea to write them together, so he probably wouldn't mind sharing.

"Can we still do our eulogies together?" she texted him.

A response popped up immediately. *"Absolutely."*

Before she could respond, he sent another. *"Meet me after work at the beach house."*

She sent him a thumbs-up and tucked the paper into her purse, hoping that his early morning response didn't mean that he was having more bad dreams.

Birdie entered Tea and Tennyson that morning like a swift wind on a still day, the kind that spread around trash and made a mess of things. "Scrunchie!" she yelled. "If I had myself a compound bow, I'd shoot Emma straight through that shriveled little heart of hers. I swear I would."

"Why are you threatening her life, Mrs. Crane?" Scruggs

answered calmly.

"I heard that she quit!" Birdie spat.

"People are allowed to quit. Just like I am quitting this conversation."

"Hush your piehole, Scrotum. I am trying to feel sorry for you."

Scruggs chuckled. "Whatever you say."

"The gall of that girl. Why does she not have the decency to tell us why she left? We deserve to have answers."

"I have no idea," Scruggs said with no emotion, working on a customer's coffee order. "It's over. Just leave her be."

"Leave her be? After what she did to you?"

Scruggs turned on Queenie's frother, drowning out Birdie's shrill voice with the noise of the coffee machine, forcing her to hold her tongue until the milk in his little metal pitcher was fully foamed. "She ghosted us, Birdie," he said. "That's all. It's, like, a common thing these days."

Krista didn't know whether to be proud of Scruggs or worried about him. She stayed out of the conversation.

"Since when did you become a sloth?" Birdie made a show of moving slowly as she drew out her words and mocked him. "I'm Scruggs and I don't care, I'm leaving her alone, whatever will be will be and la la la."

"Listen, she doesn't owe me anything. And if I find out that you stuck your nose into any of this, I tell you what"—he pointed a finger at her—"I do own a compound bow and I will use it. On you."

"As if." Birdie huffed. "You couldn't shoot a bull's-eye from two feet away." Then, to highlight her point, she crumpled up a napkin and pitched it toward the trash can, missing by a foot. "Shoot."

Krista picked up the paper and placed it in the can for her. Birdie wasn't going to retrieve it anyway.

"The truth will come out, you know," Birdie stated. "She'll say something to someone, and then it will be out there forever, waiting to be found. It's like toothpaste squeezed from the tube—ain't no puttin' it back in."

Scruggs continued to show no emotion, but surely he recognized what Birdie said as truth, just like Krista did. And Krista, of all people, knew how truth and rumors got mixed together like necklaces in a drawer, impossible to disentangle. What started out as truth, inevitably ended up as a big, hurtful lie. And they'd hear it eventually.

THERE WAS SOMETHING about Katu Island—the protected wildlife, the lush landscape, and the absence of people, that reminded Krista that there was hope for the world. There was life outside of Crickley Creek, there was simplicity and a spiritual oneness with nature that she hoped and prayed her little brother was enmeshed in—that he had wings like the brown pelican, night vision like the bobcat, ears like a little brown bat, and a nose like the black bear. That every inch of his body was at peace, working perfectly, experiencing infinite joy and intelligence, wanting and grieving for nothing.

She waited at the beach house for Johnny, staring at the now creased and wrinkled eulogy. She was still at a loss for what to write, but less concerned about the words than the fact that she was about to be alone with Johnny. Lately, his face had taken over her brain, smiling the moment she opened her eyes, leaning in for a kiss the moment she closed them, and in every pose she'd ever seen him the majority of the time in between. Never in her eight years with Rye had she thought so much about him. As a matter of fact, she used to try not to think about him as much as possible. When she heard Johnny's car pull up beside the house, her pulse quickened.

"Krista?" he called out, opening the front door.

"In the kitchen!" She grew more fidgety and nervous with every step he took.

When he entered the room, she accidentally knocked over her chair while trying to stand for his hug. He picked it up for her, then pulled her into his chest. She was grateful he couldn't see her reddening face, at least for the moment.

"You ready to do some homework?" he asked.

She sat down. "I can't think of a single dadgum thing to put down on this paper."

"I skipped over the whole *where I was born, what were my hobbies* stuff. Just answer this one question: How do you want to be remembered?"

"Can I read yours?" she asked.

He handed over a typed and printed piece of paper. "I gave Ashby the original, but I typed this in so I could look at it every now and then. You know, remind myself."

Krista looked at the page and burst into laughter. "You wrote bullet points."

"You making fun of me?" he joked.

She pinched her lips together, pretending to suppress her laughter, and shook her head. "Never."

"Give that to me." He snatched his eulogy from her and cleared his throat. "Johnny Merrick was brave. He was honorable. He loved challenges. He always put his family first. He could be counted on. He didn't take life too seriously—"

"Are all those true?" she interrupted.

"I hope so. At least, I hope they are all very true by the time I die."

"You forgot to add, 'He was very wise.'"

"Bullet point number twenty-two," he added. "He learned from his mistakes."

Even though he hadn't finished his lengthy list, he turned the paper over, leaned back, and crossed his arms. "Your turn."

"Well, you wrote some great things for me already," she said. "Thank you very much."

"You're welcome." He uncrossed his arms. "So, what

next?"

"I think I'll just add one little thing. The only thing that really matters to me."

He raised his eyebrows.

Krista picked up her pen and wrote: *She loved well.*

Chapter Thirty-Five

"I BROUGHT SOMETHING for you," Krista said, leaning down to whisper in Andy Sue's ear. She and Johnny had driven to Beaufort to meet Earl, Laura, and Andy Sue at a local park.

"Yayyyyyyyy!" she clapped. "What is it?"

"It's in my bag. Should we go find it?"

"Yes!" She jumped up and down.

Krista walked over to where she'd set her purse behind the ice chest. On the street ahead of her, a large black SUV was driving by. The windows were rolled down, and Krista caught sight of familiar red hair on the backseat passenger. It was Emma. Just as Krista recognized her, Emma turned her head. It was only a second of eye contact before the vehicle passed by, but it was enough. Emma looked like she was miserable.

Andy Sue tugged on Krista's shirt. "Where is it?"

Krista picked up her large purse and pulled out two stuffed giraffes. Both had red bows wrapped around their necks. "Since we're sisters," she said. "I thought we should have sister giraffes. Which one do you want?"

Andy Sue gasped. One was her old one-eared giraffe and the other was a fuzzy brand-new version of the same. It had taken some work to find it. Andy Sue grabbed the new one. "You get Ernie," she said, pushing the old one toward Krista. "He loves you best."

"Thank you," Krista said, kissing Ernie on the head. "I'm glad to know his name."

"And this one is…" She looked around for inspiration, her eyes landing on her mother's cup of brown liquid, "Sweet Tea."

"His name is Sweet Tea?"

"No, *her* name is Sweet Tea. And it's not Sweet Tea. It's Sweetie."

"Oooooh. Well, I love it. Ernie and Sweetie."

"Ernie is a girl, too, you know. They have to be because they're sisters."

"Of course. Short for Ernestine?"

"No, Ernie Sue." She put Sweetie's head up to Ernie's, making a loud kissing sound. "They love each other."

"They sure do," Krista agreed.

Krista joined Earl, Laura, and Johnny at the weathered wooden table in the shade where she picked up her egg salad sandwich and took a bite.

"When do you leave?" Earl asked.

"In two days," she said.

"You got a place already?"

"My boss is letting me stay in her guest room until I can

find an apartment. It'll only be a couple of days, probably. I found some options, I just haven't seen them yet."

"And you can afford them?"

"Yes, Daddy." She was irked that he asked in front of Johnny. "I have some savings, and Mama said I could pay her back if I needed more."

Earl had kept his word and paid Junie $40,000, which was evidenced by Junie's new apartment and her growing wardrobe. He'd also deeded the property over to Krista.

"Junie's pretty damned happy 'bout that load of cash I gave her." He put his hand over Laura's and she smiled at him. "Best thing I ever did." Then, to Krista's astonishment, her old daddy got teary-eyed. "Y'all are too good for me," he said. Laura handed him a napkin and he used it to dab his eyes. "I know I hardly ever say it, but I love y'all. My girls." He patted his chest twice and a sob escaped. "My three special girls."

Andy Sue climbed onto his lap and used the head of her new giraffe to wipe his tears. "Don't cry, Daddy."

"Those are happy tears," Laura said.

Andy Sue turned to Krista. "Yours, too?"

"Yes. Mine, too."

IT WAS EARLY afternoon by the time Johnny and Krista made it back to Crickley Creek. The day was so beautiful, they decided to go straight to Katu Island for a walk along the beach. There was still debris from the storm surge, some of which was above the turtle nests marked with a yellow flag. Krista prayed the eggs were still viable. They needed oxygen to survive.

Johnny was like her personal photographer, snapping photos as they strolled along the beach. During the drive back from Beaufort, they'd spent quite a bit of time talking about her social media fame. It was an opportunity, and she needed to decide if she was interested in accepting some of the brand deals that had been offered. Bill's Pro Shop had offered her two top-of-the-line fishing rods if she'd post one video about their store. She was excited about that one. She could replace Johnny's and still have a new one for herself.

There had been multiple offers of free bathing suits if she would model them and tag the company, which was an easy no. But the opportunity for real money came from companies that wanted to advertise on her YouTube channel. The offers were in the thousands of dollars. If she got just two advertisers, she could make a large down payment on a condo in Myrtle Beach. But she'd have to keep creating what Johnny called content, and she wasn't sure she knew how.

They were just turning back toward the road when they noticed movement near the dunes. It was like the sand was boiling. As they neared, the first baby loggerhead pulled itself out of the sandy nest using awkward, hard-working front flippers. Then more and more appeared, birthing themselves from the sand. It was like the beach itself had gestated this active, miraculous clutch of turtles. Johnny stood near the sea while Krista stationed herself near enough to the nest to fight off seagulls or any other predators. Together, they encouraged the babies as more than one hundred of them made their journey to their ocean home. Each time one made it through the surf and into the calm, Krista and Johnny let out a whoop.

By the time the last baby made it, they were dependent on the light from the moon to see. And they were starving. The lights were off at the beach house and the front shades were drawn, as they always were at night, to not upset the turtle's instincts to head out rather than in. They used Johnny's cell phone as a flashlight. The first thing Krista noticed was the rosebushes they'd planted. They were filled with pink flowers so light they looked white. "Look!" She knelt to the ground next to the house. "They're thriving." She leaned in and sniffed the fragrant flower, explaining to Johnny how she and Zach had transplanted them from the marsh. "Do you see this, Zachy?" she whispered.

"Maybe we can take some cuttings from these," Johnny said. "Plant them at my place."

"How about building the old garden back on my part of the marsh? I could work on it every time I visit. Surely we could get the old water lines going again. It would be for Zachy."

Johnny snapped a moonlit photo of her smelling the

sweet rose. "You are so beautiful," he said like a whispered thought, his masculine face earnest in the dusty white light of the moon.

She smiled. It felt good to hear. With Johnny, she didn't feel compelled to wear mascara or keep pink lip gloss in her pocket for constant retouching. The compliment felt more like an appreciation of who she was rather than what she looked like.

They were too hungry to take the time to cook an entire meal, so dinner was tomato sandwiches from the heavily producing plants in Charlotte's backyard planter. There was Duke's mayonnaise in the cupboard and a whole loaf of soft white bread. Charlotte had encouraged them to eat whatever she kept at the cottage.

Krista and Johnny sat on the swing on the porch, listening to the waves and the nighttime sounds, rocking in unison, eating their sandwiches, and discussing their day. He was familiar now, his musky bergamot smell and the curve of his jaw, the crinkle of his eyes and his one slightly twisted bottom tooth—they were a constant in her life. They were a comfort.

She let him push off the ground to keep the swing in motion rather than using her toes to help. Instead, he stopped it. Brushing a strand of hair from her face, he asked, "Krista Hassell, I've been wanting to ask you this for a while now. And since you're leaving soon, I want to make sure I've got you locked in." He laughed. "Will you officially be my girlfriend?"

Her heart flip-flopped like a fish on the line. She'd thought about it, of course. As much as she didn't want a long-distance relationship, she couldn't imagine living a life without Johnny. She leaned in and kissed his soft lips. "Of course I will."

"I was counting on that." He chuckled and kissed her again. "Does this mean I can tell everyone that my girlfriend is famous?"

"I'm about as famous as this here swing we're sitting on."

"It deserves every bit of the attention," he said, patting the seat. He started the soothing back and forth motion of the swing again and she pulled her knees up under her chin as she soaked in her new title, Johnny Merrick's girlfriend. It didn't come with the expectations attached to being Rye Smithson's girlfriend. It didn't come with the preconceived notions. It came with excitement and hope and possibility.

"Speaking of fame." He pulled out his phone. "Look." He showed her the video of the baby turtles and how she protected them. "Can I post it for you?"

"Yes, please," she said, watching him more than the video and vowing to make a point of enjoying every moment she got to spend with him. She had so much to be grateful for. "I have some ideas for that content stuff you were talking about," she said. "I've been spending some time learning about how it all works."

"Does that mean I don't get to be your manager anymore?"

"You can be my consultant," she said. "And photographer."

"Sounds like a demotion, but I'll take it." His smile cut straight through to her heart and set it ablaze. She took in his strong presence and his growing-out hair that was looking less and less military every day. He really was hers, and she was going to love him well.

Chapter Thirty-Six

JUNIE WALKED INTO Tea and Tennyson on Friday afternoon wearing an actual dress. And not a short one, either. It was a white eyelet sundress with full chest coverage and puffy sleeves. It may have been more appropriate for a twelve-year-old, but the fact was, Junie was trying. She'd come into the store for a job interview. With Krista leaving and Emma gone, Charlotte was in desperate need of employees.

At four P.M., Krista flipped the sign to CLOSED and locked the door. Junie was still at a corner table speaking animatedly with Charlotte. She gave her mother a thumbs-up and waved as she headed upstairs to the loft.

She'd positioned the camera so that the light from the front window made her skin glow and eyes sparkle. She expected to be nervous talking in front of a camera, having had absolutely no experience doing it. But by the time she was framed on the couch in front of Charlotte's huge ocean painting, she was ready.

The timer counted down: three, two, one.

"Hey y'all. I'm Lucky Lucy. Most of y'all have met my

friends, Blacktip the shark, Mr. Big Ole Gator, the yellow slider he tried to eat, and at least a hundred of my new loggerhead babies." She giggled. "Now I've got to thank all of y'all. See, I've been wanting to leave this amazing place that I live in for a while now. There are some *ain't you precious* and *bless your heart* people here who have looked down on my family for years. Not that they're without cause. I mean, my cousin is in jail for killing a man. But just because we're backwoods or rednecks doesn't mean we're all bad people." She shrugged.

"This summer has been a big one for me. My house got destroyed by a flood. I saw my dad again after ten years, and I found out that I have a little sister, who is awesome, by the way." She waved at the camera. "Hi, Andy Sue!" Pulling a pillow onto her lap, she continued. "But the worst part of this crazy summer is that my little brother died. I'm not telling you this for pity. What I want to do is to thank you."

More than the phone screen, she could see Johnny's face. She was talking to him.

"See, I don't want to leave Crickley Creek anymore. When y'all started paying attention, something happened to me—I started paying attention, too. It's like, not feeling good enough is just a stupid thought—and we can learn to control our thoughts. We can change those. So, thanks to y'all and to the guy who's been recording the videos, I'm staying."

She waved her hands in front of the camera. "I'm sorry.

I'm gettin' all teary-eyed." She wiped at her face with the heel of her hand. "That's it, I guess. Thank you so much for inspiring me, and for reminding me of who I am. I'll try to post more stuff that I think y'all will like. Okay, now. Bye."

She cried all over again when she watched the video. How strange that sunsetcrush, lilmackenna, zeeminator, and over 50,000 other strangers were interested in her life. There were humans behind those names, people with feelings and interests and jobs and struggles—and they had all seen her face. They had witnessed snippets of her life. And they wanted more.

She had one more thing to do.

She dialed the charity in Myrtle Beach.

Junie was sitting alone at the corner table when Krista came back down. "Hey, Mama," she said. "You're still here."

She noticed that her mother's teacup was empty. "You want a refill before we go?" She reached for the cup, but Junie grabbed her hand.

"Kiki?"

Krista melted at the name Zach had for her. "Yes, Mama?"

"Thank you for being there with Zach." Tears threatened to spill over, but it wasn't one of Junie's normal melodramas. "I feel better because you were there. Tell that Johnny that I'm glad he was there, too."

"I will." She patted her mother's hand.

"Did Zachary say anything about me? Was he upset that I wasn't there?"

"He wasn't upset, Mama." Krista pulled out the chair across from her and sat. "I think it would have been harder for him to go if you'd been there, so it was good that you weren't. He did want me to tell you something, though." She leaned in and looked her mother straight in the eye. "It was real important to him that you know he loves you."

Junie's lips shook, and she bit them together.

"And don't worry, Mama, he knows you love him, too."

"Yes, yes." She wiped at her tears. "Okay. That's good." She stood to go without leaning on Krista for help or dramatically pretending like her legs no longer worked. "I haven't been going out, you know."

"You haven't?" Krista wasn't sure whether to believe her.

"Nope. I don't even know why. I think it's 'cause the landlord showed me how to set up that Netflix thing and now I've got me some shows." She lifted her brows in surprise. "I'd just rather stay home and watch 'em. They make me happy."

"I'm glad, Mama. That's real good."

"Yeah, and I'm thinking about talking with Pastor Crane. You know, get me a little help and all."

"I think you should, Mama."

Junie hugged her tight and whispered, "And I just got me a job." She released her daughter with a smile wider than the night's sky and walked out the door toward her new downtown apartment.

"Well, I'll be," Krista said aloud. "We just switched it up. Like daughter, like mother."

Chapter Thirty-Seven

KRISTA LOOKED FORWARD to weekends the way she looked forward to good books, freshly brewed sweet tea, and fried chicken—there was nothing better. It was Saturday, and she was supposed to be packing her car for her drive to Myrtle Beach. Instead, she drove to Johnny's house. She'd posted the video that morning, and she could hardly wait to get his reaction.

With the windows of her little blue Mustang wide open, she sang along with the radio, her long hair swirling around her head. She had to work to keep her speed down, he was like a magnet pulling her in.

She hopped out as soon as she parked in his driveway and ran up the front steps to ring the doorbell. It was hard to wait. She felt like Andy Sue jumping up and down. She rang the bell again. It was eight thirty and he was an early riser; he had to be up already. She went back down the steps and peeked in through the garage door windows. His car was there. Maybe he'd gone for a run. She looked up and down the street for a sign of him. There was only a heron looking at her like she was an intruder. She ran back up the stairs and rang again. When he still didn't answer, she tried the doorknob. It twisted easily and the door came open.

"Johnny?" she said, poking her head inside. "You here?"

"Johnny?"

She heard footsteps upstairs. "Johnny? Are you home?"

A shadow filled the space at the top of the stairs and began stepping down.

"Hey, sleepyhead," she laughed.

He was wearing black boxers and his newly grown-out hair had several haphazard peaks. He rubbed his eyes. "Krista?"

"Looks like you got some sleep." She couldn't take her eyes off of him, crazy hair and all.

"Best sleep I've gotten in four years." He reached the bottom and leaned in to kiss her on the head.

"Sorry to wake you up."

"Don't be silly," he said. Then, "I really need to brush my teeth. Want some coffee?"

"I'll make it." She moved into the kitchen while he jogged back up the stairs.

When he came back down, he was dressed and wide awake. "Now, for a proper kiss," he said, pulling her to him and taking his time to press his lips against hers.

"I have something to show you," she whispered.

He pulled away, his eyes wide.

"Not like that!" She laughed. "Did you see my video?"

"You posted something?"

She pulled her phone from her pocket and found what she'd made. "Here's my little speech." She held her phone up for him to see.

"You look great," he said.

"Shhh. Listen."

When she got to the part about staying, Johnny stepped back. "What?"

She shrugged. "Oh, just that I'm not moving to Myrtle Beach today."

His mouth dropped open. "You're staying?" When she nodded, he swept her up and spun her around. "What about your job?"

"I called and asked if I could work remotely. They agreed. I only have to go in once a month for team meetings."

"Krista Hassell, you are amazing."

She grinned. "And I will be paying Charlotte rent to stay in the loft. I might fill in at the store every now and then, too, if she needs the help and if I have time."

"Well, okay, Miss Full of Surprises. Got anything else?"

"Maybe just one little thing." She coyly put a finger to her lips.

"Seriously?"

"Well, you don't have to be a part of it if you don't want."

He stared at her with a smirk.

"Daddy, Laura, and Andy Sue will be here in an hour.

We're gonna start clearing my property."

"Okaaaaay..."

"Because my daddy and I are gonna build me a house."

A slow smile spread across his face. "A house next door, huh?"

"I figure it's as good a place as any."

"It's the best place on the entire planet."

"It's going to take a long time, and it's going to be a lot of work."

"Good thing I live here," he said.

Krista was practically bouncing off the walls. "It's gonna have two bedrooms and a kitchen that opens into a family room, a big bookcase where I can put my turtle and my giraffe and the card you gave me after the wedding. There'll be a screened-in back porch, of course. And I will have a metal roof so I can hear the rain showers, plus hurricane shutters on all the windows, painted blue like the ceiling of the back porch to keep the haints out."

"You've been doing a lot of thinking and planning, haven't you?"

"It all started with that iron tub. The marsh took it from me, and now I'm gonna take it back. I'm gonna fix it up and make it good as new."

Johnny began to speak, but she put a hand over his mouth. "I know what you're gonna say. Yes, I will be raising the house ten feet. Yes, I am moving it farther away from the marsh. And yes, I will have a sea wall just like you do."

"Good," he said from underneath her hand. She pulled it away and wiped it on her jean shorts, then handed him a cup of coffee.

Krista was so antsy that Johnny only took a couple of sips before grabbing his work gloves and following her next door. There was a breeze coming off the marsh, just enough to cool off what was already another warm summer day.

"I want to start with the garden," she said. "Right here." She pointed to a patch of dirt in a natural clearing. "Now, Mama's garden used to be over there," she pointed. "And if the surge didn't take too much of the topsoil, Zachy's bulbs might still be in the ground."

Johnny began making a pile of old wood, tree branches, and trash, while Krista dug up the old garden. She cut her eyes to him often. The sweat glistening on his skin, his focus and strength and a little wiggle every now and then to the beat of the very loud music coming from the little speaker he insisted on bringing. She'd been digging in the spot where she hoped she might find some of Zach's bulbs for a while now. She sprinkled a shovelful of dirt, and a small onion-looking bulb fell out. "I found one!" She shoveled madly, uncovering two more. "They're still here!" Tiny green sprouts pushed out from the tops, as if the flood hadn't disturbed them at all and they were ready to make a fall stretch for sunshine.

By the time Earl, Laura, and Andy Sue showed up, Krista had a huge pile of flower bulbs.

Earl helped Johnny pile up the detritus while the girls kept finding bulbs. They all talked and worked and sang to Johnny's music. Just before their lunch break, Johnny and Earl disappeared. They appeared again from the patch of palmettos using all of their might to pull the beast-like iron tub from its grave.

"We got it for you," Earl yelled. The girls all ran to help, each person, even Andy Sue, held on to an edge and pulled. Johnny lifted up the front while Earl pushed from the back. "Johnny says you're gonna use this old thing," Earl said, out of breath from the exertion.

"I sure am." She was proud of that old tub. Once she got it cleaned up, it would be better than the fanciest tub at the fanciest house. It had a history. It had a story.

After some cold fried chicken and Cheerwine on Johnny's dock, they all hugged goodbye. Earl got tears in his eyes again. For a man whose only emotions used to be anger and frustration, he had grown very sensitive over their ten years apart. As he squeezed her tightly, he whispered in her ear, "You're my Lucky Lucy."

Did he know about her internet fame? She pulled away from him. "Did you say Lucky Lucy, Daddy?"

"Mm-hmm. You know, y'ain't just lucky. The haints that live here at the marsh, they ain't the evil kind. They the kind of spirits who choose only the best, the kind that don't come along too often. Ya hear what I'm saying?"

She nodded, knowing exactly what he meant. The marsh

was picky. It didn't like just anybody.

"You gotta be somethin' different, somethin' special to belong in a place like this. And that's you. Ain't no one like you."

"Thanks, Daddy." He was right. She felt it in the wise part of her soul, the intuitive part that could tell a lie from the truth, good from bad, and could sometimes even see the future.

"And I like that boy you got, too. He's a hard worker. Gonna make something of himself."

She didn't tell him that he already had. But her daddy was right. Johnny wasn't finished yet.

When everyone left, Johnny and Krista went back to his dock and sat with their feet in the water. She leaned her head on his shoulder. "Do you really like it here?"

"I do," he said softly. "Want to hear my big idea?"

She lifted her head to look at him. "You have a big idea?"

"Imagine this: Lowcountry Vet Adventures. I want to share the magic healing powers of this place. My property runs for five acres. I have the pop-up houses, and Will and Charlotte said that anyone in a wheelchair could use the beach house. I think I could actually help other veterans just by taking them fishing and hiking, for boat rides in the swamp and—"

"I could lead some of the tours," she said. "I could teach people how to fish, crab, shrimp, spot gators, make a Lowcountry boil, kayak, and identify birds and plants."

"Then we could come back here to my place for barbecues and late-night talks."

"I love it!" she exclaimed.

"I'm not trying to make money at this," he said. "I'm in negotiations to sell my business, so I don't need to. But I feel like it's what I'm supposed to do. Just like I was supposed to meet you."

A school of minnows flipped and splashed in the water right next to them. They immediately yanked up their feet. "Either there's something big down there or there's a celebration going on," she said. Raising her voice, she addressed the marsh. "What do you think? Do you like his idea?"

A cool breeze blew the hair from her face and a seagull cawed overhead. She stuck her feet back into the water. "The marsh likes your idea. And so do I."

It was still humid that evening and loud with insects, a typical dusky dog day of summer. Johnny grilled steaks, and they sat in the Adirondack chairs in the garden, full-bellied and a little bit sleepy. It was his garden now. Built with Aunt Alice's love but tended to with Johnny's.

A quick flash in the distance caught her eye. She kept watching the space to make sure she'd actually seen it.

"There!" she said, pointing to the darkness underneath a pine tree. "I see the first lightning bug of the night."

"You get the good luck," Johnny said, reaching over to hold her hand.

They watched the area for more, pointing each time another one showed up, called forth by the light of the first.

As the sun set, the bugs came closer, into the garden, among the roses.

"I hope Zach can see all the good stuff that has been going on down here," she said.

"I think he had something to do with it."

The little hairs on her neck stood up. "Do you feel him?" she asked.

"Yeah. I think I do."

She switched to a whisper, not wanting the mood to shift. "Maybe it's just the lightning bugs."

"No, I've felt him out here before."

She turned to face him. "Why haven't you told me that?"

"Didn't want you to think I was crazy."

A firefly landed on Krista's knee. "Look!" she whispered. "One landed on me." She felt connected to the little bug. "I miss you so much, little brother. I love you. I'll always love you." The bug sat with its wings raised but no light. They sat for several minutes in the peaceful stillness. It seemed neither wanted to break the spell.

At the beginning of the summer, if someone had told her she'd be sitting in Aunt Alice's garden with the crazy guy from the wedding, feeling good about herself, planning to build a house, and talking to a firefly like it was her brother, she'd have thought they were being cruel. Now, summer was almost over, she'd survived it, and the fireflies would soon disappear. She squinted at the insect's tiny black and red face and whispered, "Blink twice if you love me."

The bug's abdomen lit up as bright as the moon. Once. Twice.

Krista gasped. "Did you see that?" The bug flew into the night, dancing like in celebration, blinking in series of two.

"That could not possibly be a coincidence," said Johnny.

"We got our proof," she said, her voice barely audible. "He's whole again." The firefly flew upward instead of hovering near the ground like the rest. It soared up and up until it blended in with the starry sky. "Bye, Zachy," she said. "Thank you."

Johnny stood and pulled her up with him. They swayed to the music of the insects and the sound of marsh water swooshing slowly through the grass. "I can't believe that just happened," he said. "You okay?" His usual question.

"Mm-hmm," she purred as she inhaled his scent and put her head on his chest, his heart pumping fast and strong.

"Krista?" He kissed her on the forehead, and pulled away, rendering them nose-to-nose. "I love you," he said. "I've loved you for a long time."

The light inside of her soul shone in perfect synchronicity with his. It connected her to the universe again, to her brother, and to a little girl named Krista Hassell who'd grown up on the marsh in the South Carolina Lowcountry.

"I love you, too."

Epilogue

JUNIE HASSELL STOOD on the dock at the marina handing out life vests as the participants in Lowcountry Vet Adventures made their way onto the boat. Her ponytail shimmered in the sun as she worked her volunteer position, smiling kindly at each soldier, her army-green T-shirt announcing that it was possible to HEAL LIKE STEEL. She'd come a long way, and not only was she thriving with her day job at Tea and Tennyson, she was helping others to thrive now, too.

Will Rushton led that weekend's fishing expedition, and Charlotte had gotten him an authentic ship's captain hat that he wore as he stood near the pot haulers on the bulkhead, welcoming everyone aboard.

Krista and Johnny hosted a second group at the swamp that day—a gator hunt, they'd called it. Only they weren't hunting with guns, just their eyes. Each of them were stationed at the back of a rowboat, paddles in hand and swamp lore at the ready.

Johnny sold his company a year ago and hired marketers, psychologists, ecologists, fundraisers, and experts of all sorts to build a world-class organization catering to veterans suffering with PTSD. Virginia Buchanan was one of their biggest donors.

Krista drove to the College of Charleston three times a week to finish her bachelor's degree in psychology. She worked part-time for the Myrtle Beach children's charity, helped Johnny organize adventurous outings, and studied for school in her new two-bedroom home, built up on piers, with a large wraparound porch screened in on the backside. There was more than enough money from both her day job and her social media job in her bank account, and she rarely, if ever, thought about Rye Smithson. Every spare moment was spent with Johnny Merrick. They'd even built a crushed oyster shell pathway through the trees connecting their two homes.

Birdie was more annoying than a chigger, inserting herself into Krista's life at every turn. Not because Birdie wanted to spend time with Krista, but because she wanted her growing number of Instagram followers to know how tight she was with the most famous person in Crickley Creek. Being around Birdie was like being hounded by a paparazzi who insisted on starring in each of their ill-begotten photos.

Scruggs graduated college that spring with a degree in engineering. He still hadn't spoken to Emma, and no one in Crickley Creek had figured out why she left. It was a mystery of the past now, and was mostly forgotten.

When Krista's home was finished and the bulbs and roses

replanted, she waited until the orange, pink, red, and white blooms of the ranunculus and dahlias were as big as her hand and the delicate roses bloomed fragrant, then she invited Junie, Earl, Laura, Andy Sue, and Johnny to her new home for a celebration. It was a year to the day of Zach's death. They ate Lowcountry boil on the veranda and laughed together with corn stuck in their teeth and a pile of shrimp shells and tails in front of them. Then, when the sun was bright orange and the edge of the moon set to rise from the water, Krista, Junie, and Earl each scattered a portion of Zach's ashes around the flowers. Krista had already set some aside in a mason jar for the day when it would be her turn—when her ashes would mingle with her brother's, just like their spirits did now. Andy Sue thought the whole production was really all about her, and she made a show of brushing ashes off of petals, using her bare hands to press them into the dirt. It was the closest she'd ever get to her older brother on this side of heaven.

It was Andy Sue who saw the first firefly.

Johnny had adopted Sugar, who was curled up like a little white ball of fluff, sound asleep on his lap on the back porch swing. Krista swung with him as they watched the herons hunt for their supper. It was a scene they experienced together often. She looked at Johnny's strong profile highlighted by the yellow moon, and her heart flip-flopped at the sight of him. What a difference a year made. He said all the time how he was the luckiest man in the world, how his life wouldn't be nearly as happy without her, and how he had outthrown his coverage when he landed a girl like her.

The marsh had brought them together. And like the bald cypress trees that flourished in the nearby swamps Krista's roots couldn't be seen, but they wound together, knotting and stretching, growing intertwined with the people she loved. With each year they became more attached, and with each storm they grew stronger. With a foundation like that, even hurricanes couldn't knock them over.

The End

Don't miss the next book in the Crickley Creek series, *Christmas in Crickley Creek*!

Join Tule Publishing's newsletter for more great reads and weekly deals!

Acknowledgements

To begin, I have to express my unending gratitude to Tule Publishing, especially Jane Porter and Julie Sturgeon. This book would not exist without them. I am also indebted to so many friends who have inspired me to pursue this career. They are: Susie Barton, Sue Backer, Pamela and Keeton LeBaron, Diana Kallarias, Susie McCormac, Kim Mackey, Sherri Whiteford, and so many others who read my books and encouraged me. My sisters are my unofficial support group: Susie Herring, Holly Wenzl, Noelle Reese-Noggle, Meggan Lokken, Millie Steber, and Alice Perrins. The joy of hearing from both my mother-in-law, Sharon Reese, and my stepmother, Maureen Lokken, after they finish each book is something I live for. And my dad's belief in my abilities makes me a better person and writer.

I owe a debt of gratitude to a man known as "Cowboy." He is a boat guide at Cypress Gardens in Monck's Corner, South Carolina, and he taught me everything I know about swamps. I am astounded at the support I've received from high school and college acquaintances—shout out to the good folks from Virgil I. Grissom High School and Auburn University! I have also been blessed with the two best

Lowcountry beta readers, Dawn Lee Schaeperkoetter and Edi McNinch. I love them both as friends and as talented editors.

Finally, my heart and all of my love go to my kids: Drew and Emily Bixler, Allison Reese, Natalie Reese, and Brooke Reese. Of course, it is my husband, Bryan Reese, who is the force behind every love story I write. He will always be my hero.

If you enjoyed *Blink Twice If You Love Me,*
you'll love the next book in the...

Crickley Creek series

Book 1: *The Firefly Jar*

Book 2: *Blink Twice If You Love Me*

Book 3: *Christmas in Crickley Creek*
Coming in October 2023

Available now at your favorite online retailer!

About the Author

Photographer: Stephanie Lynn Co

Laurie Beach is a hopeless romantic who refuses to subject anyone to unhappy endings. She is a former news reporter, advertising producer, and political press secretary who, after raising four children, is parlaying her love of writing into a career as an author. Having grown up in Alabama, she especially loves novels set in the South. Laurie now lives in California with her dogs and patient husband of 26 years.

Thank you for reading

Blink Twice If You Love Me

If you enjoyed this book, you can find more from all our great authors at TulePublishing.com, or from your favorite online retailer.

CPSIA information can be obtained
at www.ICGtesting.com
Printed in the USA
JSHW080702060423
39933JS00003B/14